Glenn Patterson was born in Belfast. He is the author of six previous novels: *Burning Your Own* (1988), *Fat Lad* (1992), *Black Night at Big Thunder Mountain* (1995), *The International* (1999), *Number 5* (2003) and *That Which Was* (2004). A collection of his journalistic writings, *Lapsed Protestant*, was published in 2006. He teaches creative writing at Queen's University Belfast and is a member of Aosdána.

the third party

GLENN PATTERSON

BLACKSTAFF
PRESS
BELFAST

First published in 2007 by
Blackstaff Press
4c Heron Wharf, Sydenham Business Park
Belfast BT3 9LE
with the assistance of
The Arts Council of Northern Ireland

Reprinted 2008

Typeset by CJWT Solutions, St Helens, England

Printed in England by Antony Rowe

A CIP catalogue record for this book is available
from the British Library

ISBN 978-0-85640-809-0

www.blackstaffpress.com

For Andy, товарищ

'All right, let it end where it will,' said Don Quixote.

MIGUEL DE CERVANTES, *Don Quixote*

breakfast

1

I woke that morning, as I had woken all the previous sixteen thousand mornings of my life, as I would never wake again, knowing nothing whatever of the third party.

Another world entirely.

I hadn't bothered with the curtains so high up, so far from the office buildings opposite, so long after they had been vacated for the night. The first thing I saw as I stood naked at the window was an eagle – on my mother's grave, an eagle – sailing past two storeys below, dead straight, as though an invisible thread ran through it the length of the boulevard. Twenty storeys further below, a lone taxi, small as prey, took the curve from the road, round the ornamental gardens, to the hotel entrance. No one got out, no one came out. When I looked again the eagle was a quarter of a mile nearer its vanishing point, beyond the river. I pressed my cheek to the glass until its wings were the span of the street that in the next moment swallowed it.

Five forty-six. Four hours and fourteen minutes to my only appointment of the day. I lay on the bed, watching the window fill with light, listening to the traffic increase in volume, trying to hold at bay the thought that I could so easily not be here at all. My eyes must have closed again.

I stood up suddenly, as though propelled from a dream. No story, just pure foreboding. The knocking at my door ceased. The 'Do Not Disturb' sign was on my side, looking back at me.

'Can you come back later?' I called, rooting on the floor for shorts. I was sleep-swollen (how could a bad dream do that?), angled somewhere around a quarter past three. The clock said eight. I phoned home.

'It's midnight,' my wife said.

'I'm sorry. I woke and then fell asleep again.'

She yawned. 'Never mind.'

I tried not to. I asked about Tom. Tom would be home next Thursday. And Jill? Jill was staying at her pal's for a couple of days. (The Easter holiday had started.) She had been told, though, she was to be back for me returning.

My wife asked me was there any more biz about Our Friend Ike. The morning before last I had told her about finding him in my corridor, four floors astray, full as a lord.

'Nothing to report,' I said and my wife said she was glad for his liver's sake to hear it. She yawned again. The radio was playing low in the background. She would have it on 'sleep', distraction from the silence of an empty house.

'I'd better let you go,' I said.

'You should get his autograph.'

'What?'

'I'm just thinking, Tom or Jill might get a kick out of it.'

Tom was studying sports science. Jill was going for an A level in chat-room psychology. Ike was ... well, not chat-room material, I wouldn't have thought.

I said I'd see. I said I'd ring her in the morning from the airport.

I had hung up before I remembered about the eagle.

I showered and shaved, just showered and shaved: home tomorrow, home from my home from home. The hotel Hana wasn't the first hotel to sell itself to me this way, but it was the first to go so far as to reproduce the colour scheme of the bathroom in my parents' home circa 1978. The colours had been in and out of fashion at least once since (I was inclined to give the Hana the benefit of the doubt) and the hotel was currently undergoing another refurbishment, from the top down, or the bottom up, I hadn't been able to work out which. Part of the Skylight restaurant and bar was closed, as was the entire floor between it and me. Even the lifts were being done, one at a time, so that you couldn't be sure when you pressed the button whether the doors were going to open on yesterday's hotel or tomorrow's.

I checked my chin for shaving nicks – a bit more flesh to drag about than there was in 1978, but not, all things considered, that much – then dressed: dark grey suit, white shirt, old-gold ottoman rib tie. The cardinal rule in my line of business: the packaging is nine-tenths of the product.

The cleaning cart was half in, half out of the room opposite when I stepped out into the corridor. A disembodied brown hand rubbed a duster against its mirror image above the bathroom sink. I went back into my room for the 'Do Not Disturb' sign and hung it on the handle, 'Please Clean' side out.

I called the lift. Yesterday's.

Our Friend Ike, as my wife called him, on the basis that what was mine was hers and that I had spoken to him twice, was already in the ground-floor restaurant. I saw his room number in the register when I stopped at the entrance to show my own key to the breakfast maître d'. Wooden trellises created the effect of four separate rooms in one, the busiest, as always, overlooking the access road, narrowed here to a single lane, and the ornamental gardens beyond. Glimpses of faces were all that the trellises afforded. I didn't have to decide whether to look or avoid looking, but walked straight to an empty table next to the Western buffet, with its view inward to the kitchens, whose doors, as though magnetically opposed, never met at rest. (It was a stunt co-ordinator the waiters needed, not a maître d'.)

The buffet was continental in scope – *bi*-continental, even: Swiss-style muesli, Dutch and German cheeses, cold meats, croissants, bagels, rye bread, white and brown rolls, rollmop herrings, peppered mackerel fillets, watermelon slices, fresh fruit salad, tinned grapefruit segments, four jugs of just-squeezed juice, yoghurt, quark, cottage cheese and, rising above the rest, stainless steel hotplates heaped with hash browns, scrambled eggs, tomatoes and chipolatas.

It put me in mind of a book on medieval art I had got on trial offer from one of those clubs (I sent it back after a week) in which different scenes and even seasons were sometimes portrayed in the same painting. You had nearly to interpret the buffet before selecting your breakfast from it.

I fell in with the other chin-stroking Westerners on their slow circuit. No one wanted to be seen to make the wrong selection, the wrong interpretation. The trick was to outstay your fellows and then do a more or less blind sweep. After all, no matter how little you ate, once you had shown your key at the door you paid for everything. Or someone else paid for you. I had already had a week of croissants, rollmops, chipolatas and quark on the company's directors. I had a ten o'clock appointment. I helped myself to a small dish of fresh fruit salad and observed as I took my seat the disappointed faces of those still standing, their options, it was somehow understood, limited by my restraint.

As I was raising the first spoonful to my mouth, a finger jabbed me through the trellis at my back.

'What's the matter? Do you not speak to the poor no more?'

I turned. Ike (he no more said 'no' for 'any' than I did) grinned to fit a wooden square.

'All on your lonesome? Why don't you come round here?'

'I have a meeting at ten. I'm going as soon as I've eaten this.'

'So, eat it round here.'

'Thanks, but ...' I conveyed my meaning – and mango – with the spoon to my mouth.

'Oh, come on,' he said. 'Live a little.'

I turned to him again, focusing on the eyes this time, the next square up. Green on pink. They showed no sign of believing that I was serious, that anyone would prefer their own company to his.

I lifted my bowl. What was the point in arguing?

There was no one at the Western buffet now. It was an effort not to spear a couple of squares of Leerdammer and a brown roll in passing, scoop some scrambled egg on to a plate.

Only as I came round the far side of the partition, past the Japanese buffet, did I realise that Ike had other company. He was leaning across the table, his back to me, talking to a Japanese woman – perhaps the same Japanese woman I had seen at his table when I walked through the lobby at half past midnight – and a man, Mediterranean maybe, who sat on the other side of him in shorts, vest, and bright green running shoes. I thought there was a fair chance he had forgotten already that he had insisted I join him. I could turn back the way I had come, leave the restaurant and take the lift up to my room. I would go to my meeting, do my remaining shopping, and have a quiet dinner; and when Ike got up for breakfast in the morning – if he did get up for breakfast two days running – I would be gone. But a chance inclination of his head just then brought his profile into relief against the backdrop of the ornamental gardens, through the window at the far end of the room, and I could no more have turned away then than I could fly. My dream came back to me, all in one frame, like the medieval paintings, like the Western breakfast buffet. Ambulances, police cars, something in the undergrowth: *someone*; a hotel cleaner speaking to a reporter in perfect English, 'He was pedalling the air like it was a bicycle.'

The man in shorts nudged Ike's hand. He broke off, turned his head slowly to face me, with every degree becoming ever more certainly a part of that dreamscape.

'You look like you've seen a ghost,' he said.

You're the ghost, friend.

I shook my head and set my fruit salad on the table. 'A sudden thought,' I said.

'You want to avoid those,' Ike said and his companions smiled. 'Let me introduce you: Kimiko Saotome, Dražen Majer.'

'Kimiko,' I said and, less confidently, 'Dra–zhen.'

'I was just saying,' said Ike, rather than introduce me in return, 'you were out here fighting the good fight on behalf of Northern Irish industry.'

I reached into my pocket for cards, as much to make up for Ike's omission as anything. I gave him one while I was at it. He read the name. Dražen glanced at it once, nodded, and tapped the bottom edge on the table. Kimiko took hers in both hands and read it carefully, then set it beside her plate for further contemplation. She contemplated it so much she seemed to lose all appetite.

The food on the table was from the Japanese buffet: steamed fish and daikon, rice with flaked nori topping, miso soup and green tea.

Dražen folded his bottom lip over the top and stretched his legs out to one side, causing an oncoming waiter to improvise a hop to keep from going sprawling.

'Listen,' I said, 'don't let me interrupt you.'

'You're not interrupting,' Ike said.

'Not at all,' said Kimiko and looked at the card on the table again. Next to it was a conference pack, a picture on the cover of a pen emerging from an exploding shell: 'Writing Out of Conflict 2004'. 'Please. Sit.'

I had met Ike three evenings before. I spotted an old airport identification tag on his flight bag as I waited to check my messages at the hotel reception.

'Belfast City,' I said.

He paused filling in his registration details and looked at me over the top of his sunglasses.

'Your label. BHD. Have you been?'

I didn't make a habit of seeking out Belfast connections when I was abroad, but Hiroshima was a very long way from home. Afterwards I wondered whether the look he gave me wasn't one of annoyance that I had recognised his tag and not his mug.

'Oh, I've been,' he said, in the voice of one born there, 'and, worse, they're making me go back as soon as I'm finished here.'

'I know what you mean.' It was a perfectly pleasant April evening, twenty degrees: Hanami season, people picnicking under the cherry blossom along the riverbanks. Belfast, when I left it, was still struggling to shrug off winter. I waited while he copied out his passport number. 'So what, big aeroplanes aside, brings you to Hiroshima?'

He smiled, briefly, at the spirit behind the joke. 'Same as you, I suppose. Business.'

'What line are you in?'

'Actually' – looking at me again over the sunglasses – 'I'm a writer.'

His tone suggested it was something he should apologise for, though that's not what his eyes said.

'Newspapers?'

'Novels.'

'Ah!' I had met enough journalists to last me a lifetime, but this was my first-ever novelist. 'Anything I would have heard of?'

'Tell me the novels you've heard of and I'll stop you when you get to one of mine.'

'I'm sorry.' He had half turned away. 'You must get asked that a lot.'

'Just the odd time. What do you do yourself?' he asked. I told him: plasticised PVC packaging. 'Right, right.'

I got that a lot too, the glazed expression. I gave him a card anyway. He glanced at it. Not a flicker. Good.

'I'm on a scouting mission,' I said. 'There's a big conference here later in the year, mayors and trade delegations from all over Japan and the USA. What's it they say? "Like shooting fish in a barrel." You'd like to think you couldn't miss entirely.'

His mouth squirmed with distaste: 'they' might say it; he would not. He was here for a conference himself, he said. Writing Out of Conflict.

'That sounds interesting.'

'Yes,' he said a little absently and turned to finish registering, 'I suppose it does.' He laid down the pen and picked up his bag. 'I hope you get what you're looking for.'

'So,' he asked me at breakfast three mornings later, 'did you get what you were looking for?'

In between times I had practically had to carry him back to his room, the memory of which, however hazy, might have accounted for the increased warmth in his words now.

'Just about,' I said. I had drawn a blank at the mayor's office, but other than that ... 'And you? Good trip?'

'Ask me this time tomorrow.'

This time tomorrow, I said, I hoped to be in the air.

Ike made a *moue*. 'But what about your story?'

Dražen and Kimiko looked up at me, their interest piqued.

'This man has a great story,' Ike said. 'Or so he tells me.'

I did tell him, I'm afraid, in the lift after checking my messages. I didn't realise it was another of those things people said to him a lot.

'It's one of those you probably had to be there,' I said now.

'Ah!' Ike jabbed the air. Dražen tucked his chin into his chest. 'Backtracking already.'

Kimiko's phone rang. She looked at the number before excusing herself from the table to answer. 'Moshi moshi?'

Ike watched her go; caught me watching him.

'So,' we both said then nothing more.

Dražen stood to drain his green tea. A nipple peeped out at me from its nest of dark hair. The man was practically in his underwear.

'I should be getting ready,' he said. 'Car is coming at nine-thirty.'

Ike looked at his watch. 'Oh, right.'

'No,' Dražen said. 'Don't trouble yourself. Paper is same as I gave last year in San Francisco. A change here, a change there. Nothing substantial.'

'All the same.' Ike was holding his napkin over his plate: a towel to be thrown in.

'No, really, you have long enough day as it is.' Dražen nodded to me. 'I wish you a pleasant flight.'

He tapped Kimiko's shoulder as he passed. She turned from the window, communicated with him by means of head and hand gestures, talking into the phone all the while, then turned to face outside once more.

'You run into each other often at these things, do you?' I asked.

'Me and Dražen? From time to time.'

The napkin was back in the lap. Ike picked up a little seaweed roll, a Hiroshimama.

'Cravat,' he said and ate.

'I beg your pardon?'

'*Hrvat.* The Croat for Croat.'

'Ah.'

'He's a national hero.'

I turned to catch a final glimpse of Dražen's running-vest through the trellises. I thought better of asking what it was he had done, or whether national hero was higher than intangible cultural asset, which was how Ike had asked to be addressed the night I found him staggering about my corridor. Intangible Cultural Asset Number 13, to be precise. (My wife, *hooting* through my telling of it, misheard Asset as Icon, which she and now I had shortened to Ike.)

Kimiko returned, phone held flat in her palm, at full arm's length, as though it contained something not altogether pleasant. Ike asked if everything was OK.

'Yes, yes,' she said, with a glance in my direction, and drew the arm in.

'Not more …?' He waved a hand in the air, forefinger cocked, as though spraying air freshener. She shook her head determinedly. I ate my fruit salad. I wish I could say I savoured every mouthful, but I sensed Kimiko was reluctant to talk with me there. Even bolting I wasn't quick enough. She was excusing herself again, gathering her bag, her phone, her conference pack, my card.

'Call me when you want a car to the university,' she told Ike, who stood and pulled her in for a kiss on the cheek. 'I can have it here for you in' – turning the other cheek – 'twenty minutes.'

Ike waited till she was out of earshot. 'Do you always have that effect on people?' he asked, indicating the empty seats to the left and right of him.

'I told you I didn't want to be interrupting,' I said. 'I was quite happy sitting round there on my own.'

'Oh, give over. I'm only having you on.' He ate some more, hunched over his bowl (he had the posture off pat), then looked up at me suddenly like he had forgotten for the moment I was there. We were eye to eye a second too long. I was afraid I was about to tell him something I would regret.

'I saw an eagle this morning,' I said instead, without notice to myself.

He narrowed his eyes; no pink now, no green even. 'Is this a joke? I say "an eagle?" and you say – I don't know, whatever their names are – one of the Eagles?'

'No.'

'An *eagle* eagle?'

'Gliding up the middle of the street.'

He chewed it over. 'No,' he said.

'What?'

'Impossible.'

'I'm telling you.'

'I'll ask Kimiko.'

'Kimiko wasn't there.'

'Maybe you're not.'

'Not what?'

'There. All. Quite.'

I pushed my chair back. 'Tell me, is there a lot of training involved?'

'For writing novels?' By the look on his face this was another FAQ.

'For being a complete prick,' I said.

It was a long, long walk out of the restaurant. His forced laughter pursued me, past the Japanese buffet, past the Western buffet, if anything grew louder the further away I walked. People were watching me, like *I* was the one had done something wrong. I considered stopping at the door, yelling at him to grow up, but he got his retaliation in first: 'Take a joke, will you!'

I didn't look, but I wouldn't have been surprised if he had been standing on his seat aiming at me over the trellises.

2

The cleaning cart was half in, half out of my room. The duster clung to its bathroom-mirror-image through all the convolutions of the disembodied brown hand. I looked at my watch, not because I was running late, not because anyone could see me, but because you have to do something and the repertoire, as I understood it, ran from looking at your watch, through playing with your room key, to walking back down the corridor. I played with my room key. I walked back down the corridor towards the lifts and studied the numbers above the doors, trying to guess where they would stop. The lift on the left began the countdown from twenty-five, the Skylight restaurant and bar. My eyes followed its progress, left to right, and carried on beyond zero, until they came to rest on the emergency exit sign above the fire door. A little green man silhouetted against a white rectangle, running for his life. They loved him here, that little green man. There were T-shirts, baseball caps, cartoon piss-takes: Little Green Man as the Saint, Little Green Man breasting the finishing tape …

A door closed. My door. I turned to see the front wheels of the cart reverse into the next room along.

My toothbrush and razor were aligned on the tiled ledge above the sink. The tea and coffee had been replenished. The bed might have been ironed.

I looked at my watch, switched on the laptop, running through the room repertoire; picked up the book from my bedside table. The Japan External Trade Organisation *Trade and Labelling Handbook* for 2003. I had highlighted page one, line one: 'Labels are mini-reports on products.' The handbook's own label, a jacket of turquoise pinstripe on white, reported that no JETRO money had been squandered on design. It was a theme carried through to the JETRO offices, in the Chamber of Commerce, which had the look of an overstretched job centre from several decades pre-PC. What computers there were seemed recent additions, to be squeezed in how they could among the piles of paper and the products awaiting JETRO approval. It was a bit of a shock after the Tokyo headquarters. It was a bit of a shock after Belfast, come to that. Even the minute hands of the clocks – set to the hour of business centres across the globe – were out of sync.

My eyes strayed back to the bed. When I was a student, living in halls, I would slip out of my clothes and in between the sheets the moment the cleaners had finished in my room. The aim was not to let the sheets come untucked. I would lie there for an hour, sometimes more; sometimes I would sleep; mostly I just let myself drift. I had no idea where it came from, this impulse. It didn't feel sexual exactly. Any movement at all would have spoiled the effect. Even at night, if I was careful – if my dreams were peaceful, or the drink in the Union bar had been plentiful, if I took care of my other bed-needs in the bathroom beforehand or, all too rarely, in someone else's bed – I could slip in and out for half the week before the sheets lost their fresh-laundered grip on me.

The laptop beebomped. Mail. Norma was working late at home on next week's diary. Norma, I had only discovered since I had been here, often worked late at home. The hour after her boyfriend went to bed, she said, was the most productive of the day.

I answered her queries. Yes to this meeting at this time, Tuesday, no to that conference call at that on Wednesday. I added a line about last night's dinner: okonomiyaki. I had been adding lines about my dinners since Tokyo. Norma, I had also discovered, was interested in food, over and above what the job demanded. (The job demanded only that we come up with new and better ways to wrap the stuff.) Her boyfriend, she said, wasn't in the least bit adventurous.

No, neither was my wife.

Did I find it as frustrating as she did?

Yes (I hadn't mentioned my Western buffet breakfasts), I did.

I had floated the idea of lunch when I got back, to thank her for all the extra hours while I was away, and then with the whole sorry Sardinia business before that.

Belfast could now boast three noodle bars. We could probably live without an okonomiyaki bar: the speciality of the Hiroshima region turned out to be a species of giant noodle pancake, smothered in what tasted like ersatz HP sauce. There was a mini tower block downtown – 'the okonomiyaki village' – that sold nothing but. Tonight, I told Norma, would be totally tempura. A few minutes later her reply came through. *Think of me at home with Darren and his chops!*

And, with a certain heaviness of heart, I let myself.

I showered again.

It was nine fifty-seven when I stepped out of the lift and into check-out hell: bellboys running this way and that, remotely controlled by the bell captain, hollering from his station just inside the hotel doors; two separate parties of Korean pensioners being marshalled by their tour reps either side of a trolley on which all their luggage had mistakenly been lumped together; Americans, rising above it all, repeating the fail-safe American attention-grabbing phrase, 'Excuse me. Excuse me.'

I had reserved a table in the lounge at the rear of the lobby, before the in-house nail-parlour-cum-jewellers. The steps up from one to the other might, at this time of day, have been a gender divide, though from early evening, when the Pianola played and cocktails took the place of coffee, things became a lot more fluid.

The waiter placed two leatherette coasters on my table. I took from my briefcase the little flag I carried for occasions such as this, stamped with the company's name. I read over my papers, glancing every so often towards reception, where with much noise and attempted interventions the bags were being unloaded from the Koreans' trolley: one on this side, one on that. At ten past ten my phone rang. *Terribly sorry, have been trying to get hold of you ...*

'Yes, yes,' I said. 'No, I perfectly understand. Tomorrow, I'm afraid, is no good. No, tomorrow I fly home. Yes, no, I do, I understand. These things ... we can keep in touch, and I will, I'll be back in the autumn. Yes, yes. I'll see you then. Yes, OK, no, right, OK, bye.'

I tossed the phone on the table. So much for that.

I gathered up my papers and was bending to put the flag back in my briefcase when I sensed someone by my side. I sat up quickly.

'Do you mind?' Ike rested a hand on the back of the empty seat.

I shook my head, too staggered by the sheer *neck* of him to say anything. He sat.

'I'm sorry,' he said. 'Earlier, if I overstepped it.'

I shook my head again. He nodded, picked up the menu.

'No, I didn't really think I had. I said to myself probably just, with the work and all, you were a bit wound up.'

I let out a laugh, which was lost in the uproar of one of the

Korean groups heading for the doors, where their bus had drawn up.

'Should we have coffee, do you think?' He had replaced the menu and set his maroon flight bag on the tablecloth beside it. There was the label that had got us both talking. BHD.

'Listen,' I said, 'I don't know about you, but I have things to do.' I pushed my chair back. 'So, please, go ahead, order coffee if you want, but not for me.'

He looked at his watch. 'Sorry, I thought I remembered you saying you had an appointment at ten o'clock. I thought maybe you'd been let down.'

I rested my briefcase on my lap. At least he hadn't said stood up. 'No, well, there was a last-minute change of plan.'

'That's a pain.'

'It can't be helped.'

He was making a signal to the waiter.

'All the same,' I said, 'I have things I need to be getting on with.'

The waiter arrived.

'Two coffees,' said Ike, with the faintest of interrogatives.

'One.'

Writer and waiter both looked at me.

'One,' I said again. '*Ichi.*' The waiter bowed, the writer shrugged.

'Tell us this,' he said when the waiter had gone, 'did you make it out to Mount Ogon-zan while you were here?'

'Ogon-zan? No. I took the skywalk up to the other one: you know, with the art gallery on it?'

He nodded. 'Ogon-zan's meant to be the one to see. I was thinking of trying to do it this morning.'

'What about the conference?'

'I'm not doing anything till this afternoon. I just rang Kimiko, she's sending someone with a car. They'll not mind me taking a race out there first. It's only the other side of town.'

That much was true. When I wasn't being distracted by giant

birds, I could glimpse the crest of it from my window. It looked modest enough, despite the claims I had heard for it. Still.

'It would be an opportunity,' he said.

There was no denying it would be. I didn't get up from my chair. The waiter returned with the coffee.

'I'll just have to pop up to the room,' I said, standing at last.

Ike took a stack of broken-looking books from his bag. There were Post Its between the leaves: yellow, orange, pink. 'Sure, whatever. We've twenty minutes yet.'

A second bus had arrived out front. The congestion was moving from the lobby to the pavement. ('Excuse me. *Excuse me*,' an American raised his voice, like you've done it now, you've pushed me to a full sentence. 'Can we get some service here?') I turned at the lifts and saw Ike, flight bag on the table, head down, reading himself.

After our first meeting I had checked him out on Amazon: dot-co-dot-uk, not dot-com. Two novels, ranked ninety- and a hundred-and-fifty-something-thousand. I read the publisher's descriptions. They sounded like the sort of thing I would normally run a mile from, i.e. they featured the words Northern and Ireland in close proximity. Northern and Ireland and the inevitable fruit of their union in print, the Troubles. There were six other titles, some of them listed more than once, none of them currently able to be offered.

Ninety- and a hundred-and-fifty-something-thousand. What was that? Hopeless? So-so? Not half-bad?

One of the books I had in fact heard of. I just didn't know it was by him. I thought it was by the other guy, whose name I had temporarily forgotten too. *Hurts*, 1998. 'A writer,' said its single online reviewer (four stars), 'who leaves you wondering what he will do next.'

He was still reading when I returned, a quarter of an hour later, having ditched the briefcase in my room and changed out of my suit.

He looked up at me, eyebrow arching.

'Don't tell me,' I said (people often did), 'it takes years off me.'

He didn't. I sat, doubly self-conscious. His own suit, unless I was much mistaken, was the one he had been wearing when he checked in – on the night I found him drunk in my corridor – last night as he held court in the lobby. It *looked* like wool, from some particularly hardy strain of sheep perhaps, though before it was a material, certainly before it was a style, it was a colour: black. A black suit. You could travel in it, fall flat on your face in it. Dust yourself down and stick on a tie, you could present yourself to the Queen in it.

He spoke out the side of his mouth. 'Your label's showing.'

'Say honest.' It was the oldest joke in the book. The label was stitched to the seam of my jacket's patch pocket. Paul Smith.

'Really,' he said and pointed at his collar. I turned away, scratching the back of my neck and right enough there was the label, sitting proud.

A young Japanese guy in jeans and hooded top was watching us from the front of the lounge. He started forward at the same moment as I muttered my thanks to Ike.

'Is this your driver?' I said then.

Ike rose, peered at him. 'Must be.'

The youth smiled as he drew near, tugging at the zip of his top to reveal a T-shirt emblazoned with the shell and pen device. 'Friend', it as much as said. His bow was instinctive, at once smart and loose-limbed.

'Did you sleep well?' he asked, eyes for Ike alone.

Ike gave the cagey response of a man for whom a query about sleeping was either a veiled criticism of his conduct preceding it, or the prelude to a more onerous request now. 'Reasonably.'

'Good,' said the young man and, for the first time, looked at me.

I knew better than to rely on Ike. I gave him my name and my card as back-up.

He bowed again – 'Tadao Murayama' – then turned back to Ike. 'Please, let me say, you spoke very well at last night's session. I have never read the *Iliad*, but I will read it now.'

'Ah, well.' Ike, who had been about to say something else, rearranged his expression. 'There are only two types of people in the world: those who have and those who have not.' So at least I knew where I stood. He flicked a thumb at me. 'I was saying to my friend here, we could maybe take a spin out to Mount Ogon-zan.'

'Ogon-zan?' Tadao seemed uncertain.

'If you don't mind me coming too,' I added.

'Of course he doesn't,' said Ike. He slung his bag across shoulder and started for the entrance. 'Why would he?'

'Sorry,' said Tadao. 'It is OK. My car is small, that is all.'

'Oh, look,' I said, but Ike called back: 'Come on.'

A bellboy raced us to the door, as though being paid by the metre per second.

Two luxury buses – one gold and white, the other white and gold – were parked nose to tail in the bright sunlight before the hotel and as we came out an exchange of stray Korean pensioners was being conducted midway between their front doors. Immediately behind the second, looking for all the world like a pellet of luxury bus poo, sat a tiny black car. Tadao jogged ahead of me, past Ike.

'One minute, please.' He had just leaned in to clear the back seat when I saw, over the roof of the car, movement in the ornamental gardens. Three, four people, wearing bright green aprons, carrying sacks. I blinked and they disappeared, only for half a dozen more to pop up to the left and right. Then they too bent out of sight and the first four reappeared with three others I hadn't spotted before. They advanced in a ragged, bobbing line, scouring the undergrowth.

'What on earth is that?' Ike said, and only then was I certain that the whole thing wasn't a flashback to my dream. The figures were emerging now from the gardens – bending, lifting, bagging – and I was able to make out the legend on their aprons. White letters, roman script: 'Smokin' Clean'.

'It is the time of year,' said Tadao. 'Hanami. The blossom is beautiful so long as it stays on the trees.'

He was holding the driver's seat down for me. I ducked in and nearly collided with Ike, coming from the other side, as though it was a taxi we were getting into.

'I thought you were getting in the front,' I said and then, as he was already hunting for the seat belt, backed out and went round to the passenger door.

Tadao, if he was dismayed, did well not to show it. He asked me as we pulled away if this was my first time in Hiroshima.

'Yes,' I said. 'First time in Japan.'

'Mind what you say.' Ike's voice sounded as though it was coming from somewhere close to the floor. 'He'll try and sell you something.'

Tadao's brow wrinkled.

'Don't listen to him,' I said. 'He has a very confused idea about business people.'

We had turned left out of the access road, then almost immediately right, off the boulevard, into unknown territory for me, whose business had been confined to the main shopping district, north of the hotel. We passed a pet parlour and, a little further along, the Institute of Hairdressing. I was trying to construct a witty comment, but already Tadao was hitting the indicator again and the moment, like the parlour, the institute, the street itself, slipped away. Shortly afterwards we crossed a river, one of the six – or was it seven? – that flowed through downtown Hiroshima. As much for something to say – for the silence had begun to feel uncomfortable and nothing was forthcoming from the back seat – I asked Tadao which this was.

'*Eto-ne*,' he said: let me see. He looked in the rear-view mirror. 'Enko-gawa? Kyobashi-gawa?' He shook his head. 'My mother knows them all.'

'Have your family always lived in Hiroshima?'

He nodded. 'Parents, grandparents' – a pause – 'great-grandparents.'

'I see.' I thought I did. He was twenty-ish, parents – what? – maybe forty-five, fifty; grandparents teenagers in ... well, *then*. And great-grandparents?

Of course the pause may just have been his search for the English term. Or the right turn he had been trying to make.

Ike sat forward, angled towards my right ear.

'Come here,' he said. 'Have you noticed anything? The streets, I mean.'

I looked through the windscreen at them: broad, sunny, bordered by low-rise shops. A minute before we had stopped at lights alongside a pachinko parlour clad in artfully distressed tin. 'Cool', said the sign.

'Midwest?' he prompted.

'Japanese?'

He tutted.

'Right. *American*. Can't say I've ever been.'

'Or the west coast. I noticed it coming in on the train as well: all those wee towns snaking up the canyons. Pure Californian.'

'Mm,' I said. I was watching out the corner of my eye for Tadao's reaction; great-grandson of his great-grandparents.

'I much prefer the east coast,' Ike said.

'Can't say I've been there that often either.'

'I spent a month in upstate New York a few years back. Writers' retreat.' He whistled. Hiroshima was passing like an unwatched film. A streetcar briefly came abreast – the last throw of the special effects dice – then peeled off to the right. 'If you ever get the chance to go to upstate New York in fall, take it.'

Fall? I spoke past him to Tadao. 'Do you travel much yourself?'

He smiled. 'I was in Ireland two summers ago.'

'Really? Where?'

'Limerick.'

'Lovely Limerick,' said Ike, unlovingly.

'Did you get to see much of the island?'

'No, not so much,' said Tadao, the smile gone. 'Too little time. Also I was there for a very specific reason.'

'Language school?' I asked.

'Last time I was in Limerick,' Ike cut across his reply, 'there was near a fucking riot.'

That 'fucking' sounded so harsh, so uncalled for in the little black car.

'Something you said?' I asked.

I could almost hear his face stretch itself into a mirthless smile.

'A wedding in another part of the hotel where I was reading. The two families had been feuding for about five hundred years. Ended up chasing each other round the corridors. Then the Guards arrived and the families ganged up and started chasing them. It was like one of those god-awful Irish films: "Sure, we're all mad feckers here, but it's gas, really."'

Tadao checked the mirror again. The streets were narrower now, already beginning to wind and climb.

'I'm sorry,' I said. 'It must be hard for you having to concentrate on driving and speaking English at the same time.'

'There's many a one at home has difficulty with it,' said Ike, better-natured, sitting back again.

'It's OK,' Tadao said. 'Just now and then ...'

He raised a hand from the wheel to demonstrate uncertainty then replaced it, sharpish, as another bend hove into view. Soon they were coming every couple of hundred yards. Tadao hit a rhythm: accelerate, brake, turn, accelerate, brake, turn, chatting to me between manoeuvres about his thesis, 'Healing the Hurts' (no acknowledgement of the compliment from behind): 'Literature's Lessons for Peace'; accelerate, brake, turn, accelerate, brake, turn ...

'Look out!'

I slapped my hand on the dashboard seeing a man in an orange boiler suit step into our path, waving a white flag.

Tadao touched his brake more firmly – 'Road works,' he said – but it was the flag-waving man who stopped, not us. Other men leaned on their shovels at the side of the road as we cruised by. Chestnut faces and forearms. One or two raised a hand in salute. I nodded, as anyone would have. The last man in the gang nodded back and added a wink and a smile so odd that I did a double take. He smiled and winked again, as if to say, You got here, then?

At the next corner stood another man with a red flag. As soon as we were past he strode into the road and began waving it.

'How does that flag system work?' I asked Tadao, or thought I did, for he kept looking dead ahead: accelerating, braking, turning, accelerating, braking, turning.

I was trying to see in the wing mirror if there was anything getting through behind us. The bends in the road had for a while disguised the extent of our climb. Now, though, the strain on the engine had begun to be audible. The mountain might not have looked like much from my hotel room, but through the gaps between the houses the city appeared suddenly diminished and depopulated. Only motor vehicles caught the eye: buses, taxis, Hiroshima's endless variations on the tram genus. Up here, too, things had a stripped-down look. First footpaths went, then front yards. Washing flapped its arms close to the roadside. A family of trainers – daddy, mummy, two baby pairs – aired on a low wall next to a vending machine (for there were no shops now either). And still we climbed, beyond the line of the houses, with only the inevitable cherry blossom for company and in places not even that, just a rail between us and the tumbling undergrowth. I had a moment, realising we had not seen another car ahead of us since the road works, when panic threaten to overwhelm me. I thought I would have to ask Tadao to stop and let me out of the car, of whatever it was I had stumbled into here. Then, suddenly, round another bend, there was a car park, two-thirds full. There were snack carts, Portaloos. There were people.

I had a cramp in my left hand where I had been gripping the door handle. I wound down the window with my right, breathed in: cherry blossom and salt water.

'The Inland Sea is just on the other side of the trees,' Tadao said, as though picking up the scent of my thoughts. 'We can walk higher if you want to see more. We can walk almost to the top.'

'We didn't come all this way to look out the car window,' Ike said and tapped the back of my seat.

I stepped out and almost fell to my knees. My feet had cramped up too, toes inside my shoes curled around nothing at all.

Tadao apologised again for the size of the car and in the circumstances it seemed easier to let it take the rap.

'Don't worry,' I said stoically.

Ike had taken out a leather-bound notebook held shut by an elastic band, which he now slipped over his hand while he patted his pockets for a pencil or pen: a signal, I decided, that Tadao and I should go on a few paces ahead of him. Again, Tadao did well to hide his disappointment and I did my best to compensate by asking him to explain each newly revealed sight on our short, twisting ascent: the expressway, far to the west, boring a hole in some other mountain en route to the university; the sprawling Mazda factory in the lee of Ogon-zan; the road stilt-walking past it across the bay, to Kure or Kumano, Tadao said, his mother could tell me; the docks, the docks and the islands beyond – free-floating mountains, losing themselves in the mid-morning haze.

'It's some size,' I said.

'In Japan we say *hyaku man toshi*,' said Tadao: 'City of a million people.'

'*Hyaku man toshi*,' I repeated. 'Belfast times three.'

'Limerick times ten.'

Now there was a thought to gladden Ike's heart.

At some point, not far from the summit, I realised we had lost him completely. I gave him a minute, then backtracked a few dozen yards and found him, right up against the guardrail, gazing off towards the city centre. He had put on his sunglasses, the sort my father used to pick up for a pound beside the filling-station till before long car journeys.

'This is the view,' he said.

'It's amazing, all right.'

'No, the famous one, in the Hirayama painting. The *Holocaust*?'

I must have been expected to speak.

'Don't tell me you've been here all this time and not seen it.'

'No,' I said. 'Yes. I mean …'

'This must be where Hirayama stopped when he was fleeing the city. I'll bet you any money.' He was framing the view, the notebook strapped once more to the back of his left hand: a little leather shield. In the deep distance a shinkansen – bullet train – slipped, white as a tapeworm, out of Hiroshima station. He unstrapped the notebook, fished the pencil out again, tapped it twice on the open page, once on his teeth.

'Have you a camera?' he asked.

'The battery was low. I'd to leave it in the hotel room, charging.'

I don't know if he actually rolled his eyes, but his eyebrows appeared briefly above the sunglasses frames: two black humps. 'What do you call that fella, again, driving us?'

'Tadao?'

'You wouldn't …?' he started to ask, then, seeing my face, obviously decided he was right, I wouldn't. 'Wait here a second.' He touched my arm in parting, as though entrusting the view to my safekeeping. '*Tadao!*'

I stood with my back to the city another few moments, arms folded, like an open-air bouncer, then caught myself on and turned to look at it head-on.

3

There are two versions of the *Holocaust in Hiroshima* in Hiroshima city. I hadn't been able to find the one in the Prefectural Art Museum. I had got there late in the day, the attendants were closing each gallery as I left it (bye-bye Dali, so long Arts and Crafts of Japan and Asia), and anyway, I was told afterwards, the painting was only on display in summer. The second version, made up of six enormous ceramic panels, was in the basement of the A-Bomb Museum, on a spit of land between two rivers, a ten-minute walk from my hotel. I would have missed this one too if the ground-floor toilets hadn't been being cleaned, or at least if there hadn't been a woman wandering around in there with a cloth and spray. (Japanese men, I had already noted, had no great demands when it came to privacy: the cupped hand, a urinal's porcelain wings. I could envy them, but still something in me baulked.) I had asked an attendant, who directed me to the toilets in the basement and there, at the bottom of the stairs, was the *Holocaust*: a sea, I thought, then corrected myself, seeing the husks of buildings huddled at the foot of the picture – a *sky* of flames. From one end to the other, not a single inch of breathable air.

Just looking at it left you gasping.

I sank down on to a bench before it. Shrank down.

They say no one can leave Hiroshima without visiting the A-Bomb Museum at least once. This was my third time. The first had been with Haraguchi-san from the Chamber of Commerce, though I could have gone with any one of half a dozen people I met there, since they all offered before I was in the offices an hour. Maybe it was the view: the front windows overlooked the old Industrial Promotions Hall, part of which had withstood the blast to become known the world over as the A-Bomb Dome. (The left side of the Chamber overlooked the Municipal Baseball Stadium and, sure enough, I had two offers of tickets from offices on this side if I fancied taking in a game while I was in town.)

Haraguchi-san was clearly a veteran of museum tours. Before we were even in the door he had conjured for me the once-bustling neighbourhood now occupied by the museum and surrounding Peace Park, whose northern extremity, the T-shaped Aioi Bridge, had been the A-bombers' target on the morning of 6 August 1945. Inside, he insisted on paying the entrance fees and the three hundred yen more for the hire of a headset for me to listen to an English language commentary. No sooner had I switched the headset on, however – before an artist's impression of the Edo period Hiroshima Castle – than I had to switch it off again, while Haraguchi-san, reading from the caption printed, in English, to the side of the picture, told me this was an artist's impression of the Edo period Hiroshima Castle. I thanked him, put the headset back on. He started talking again. And so it went on, through the granting of city status and Hiroshima's strategic importance in the first Sino-

Japanese War, to the glory that was the Higher School of Education, from which graduates were sent to every outpost of the growing empire.

On the occasions that he did allow me to listen without interruption, Haraguchi-san appeared to be lip-synching. The second the woman's voice in my ear had finished speaking he would be steering me on to the next exhibit, one hand open ahead of him, one hand hovering around the small of my back. He was the nicest man and, like the museum itself, couldn't have been more contrite about Japan's own wartime record. 'Japanese people were very cruel in China,' he said, before an image of a lantern parade through the streets of Hiroshima to celebrate the fall of Nanking. 'Very cruel.' All the same, he made the whole museum experience even more gruelling than I had been steeling myself to expect.

'Yo!'

Ike had returned with Tadao in tow.

'Thingy here has one of those phones with the camera and all in it.'

Tadao waved it at me. A little silver compact. I recognised the model. Camera was the least of its 'all': it was an FM radio, MP3 player, with full internet capability … More than recognise it, I knew the spec inside out. I had two of them boxed and wrapped in my hotel room: one for Tom, one for Jill; but I was still of an age where I never saw them flipped open without thinking *Star Trek*. (A sign, said Tom, that I was way too old for one of my own.) Tadao flipped his, held it at arm's length pointed at Ike, who had taken up position, leaning against the rail. I let myself imagine him vaporising before my eyes.

'Hold on,' he said and took off the sunglasses. He passed a hand vaguely over his hair and suit jacket. 'OK.'

'Cheese!' said Tadao. Ike's expression curdled. Tadao snapped and, still wearing his own cheesy grin, showed him the picture. Ike nodded: it would do.

'I can email it to you if you give me your address,' Tadao said.

Ike hesitated, as though this part of the transaction had not occurred to him till now.

'Or' – it was hard to say whose embarrassment Tadao was speaking to cover – 'I can send it to my computer at home, print it out there.'

Ike brightened. 'It wouldn't be putting you to a whole lot of trouble?'

'No.' Tadao too was smiling again. 'No trouble at all.'

'I know,' I said. 'Why don't I take one of the two of you?'

Tadao let out a long *O* sound that began in delight and ended in uncertainty. Could I … could he … possibly …?

'Of course,' Ike said, to Tadao, to me. The sunglasses were back on and, this time, were not removed.

Tadao showed me which button to press and ran back to the rail. He dinked his head to one side and made a peace sign.

Ike flinched. 'What are you doing?'

Tadao looked himself up and down, arriving at his right hand almost as an afterthought.

'This?' he said, holding up the fingers.

'That.'

Tadao's fingers wilted. 'It is just a thing people do.'

Not just people: on the way to Hiroshima from Tokyo I had seen a plaster Statue of Liberty, above a hotel entrance, hold up two enormous, cartoon-like fingers. It was halfway to a national symbol.

'*Ready?*' I said.

Ike prodded the bridge of his sunglasses. Tadao reproduced the smile, brought up the same two fingers.

I stopped, distracted, squinted past the camera. Shinkansen again, coming into the distant station.

'Don't be all day about it,' Ike said.

'Sorry.' I trained my squint on the screen again and pressed the button. 'I *think* that worked.'

Ike had started to say something else, but on the screen he

remained as tight-lipped as he had been five seconds before. I looked at it harder … Tadao reached over and took the phone from me. Another *O*: pure delight this time. He was happy anyway. He waved the picture in front of Ike, who nodded almost before he had seen it.

'What time is it?' he asked.

'Nearly half eleven,' I said.

'I need a tea or a coffee or something.'

Tadao had already started back towards the car, thumbs going at the phone.

'I am sending the pictures now,' he called to us. 'I will have them for you tonight.'

Ike had stopped again to write in the notebook: Tadao's promise, or his duty-free shopping list, for all I knew, but it was a good pose all the same. I spotted a couple of Japanese tourists taking sneaky snaps. You didn't have to know who he was to recognise what he was.

I ducked into a Portaloo before we left. It would just be like me to get the urge to go the second we were out of the car park. Forget the *Iliad* – as the doctor who examined me said, the only types of men in the world are those who have prostate problems and those who are going to have.

Tadao made the descent with his foot resting on the brake, now a touch more pressure, now a touch less. It was hot in the tiny black car and I had woken very early. Twice his braking jolted my eyes open. Each time I glanced to the side to see had he noticed, but Tadao was concentrating on the road again. The second time Ike was talking – to which of us wasn't entirely clear – about some other writer, whose name I hadn't caught, who had once on a flight to Australia for the Adelaide Festival, after a few too many complimentary gin and tonics … My eyes went again. Jolted open. Only when the road levelled out did I realise they had been closed long enough for me to miss the road works. A quarter of a mile on, we stopped at a patisserie, which looked as though it had been beamed up by powerful clamshell phone from the Europe of the later Habsburgs. Hiroshima was full of them: the Mozart, the Zurich, the Osteria, their decor only slightly less ornate than their cakes.

Whether it was the cakes or the candelabras, this one appeared to be particularly popular. Tadao went in ahead of us to see if there was a table.

A trolley passed on the far side of the glass: a dietitian's nightmare.

'Watch now you don't spoil your lunch,' I said, in my best Belfast Mammy tones.

'Lunch?' Ike snorted. 'It'll be a bento box from the university canteen. Between you and me, a bit of something now wouldn't go amiss. Anyway, I hardly eat at all in the daytime when I'm at home.'

Judging by the strain on the buttons of his black suit jacket, he hadn't been home in a while.

'I'm not going to ask are you working on something at the minute,' I said. 'Like asking a plumber or a lawyer, I suppose. Why wouldn't you be?'

He nodded: I was learning.

'Novel?'

That was a question too far.

'Sorry,' he said. 'I'm one of those people thinks it's bad luck to talk about it before it's written.'

'Of course.' I was the same way with business deals, if he had thought to ask me. 'I completely understand.'

Tadao came out. 'We can all fit in if we ...' He couldn't think of the word, so he did the action, arms rigid against his side.

'Squeeze?' I said. 'Well, listen, don't go doing it on my account. I'm going back into town.'

'Already?' Ike asked.

'It's my last day. I've still a couple of things to pick up.'

'At least wait and get a lift.'

Tadao, finding himself volunteered, had no option but to repeat the offer. 'Yes, I can take you back there.'

'Thanks, but I'm fine walking.'

'It's quite far, half an hour. You might be better taking a tram.'

'You must be joking,' Ike said. 'Tram? He's a businessman. He doesn't know the first thing about public transport.'

I took a step back to give him the full benefit of my disbelieving look. 'You can't help yourself, can you?'

He shrugged. I walked.

lunch

1

And I walked.

And walked.

It was much further than I had bargained on. Further even than Tadao had suggested. (I should have asked him to ask his mother.) It took me the best part of an hour to reach the city centre and the conjoined-quad department stores: Sogo, Aq'a, New Sogo and Pacela.

I had been in these stores any number of times since my arrival in Hiroshima and still got so lost in their interconnecting walkways that occasionally I had to make for the street and start all over again.

Akimi, the young woman from marketing who had greeted me there on my first visit, advised me always to aim for the doors beneath the Sogo clock.

'This is a traditional meeting place for Hiroshima people,' she said.

Traditional, I took it she meant, since the opening of Tokyo Disneyland, whose name was engraved in the bottom left-hand corner of the clock-face. The minute before I had met Akimi, at ten o'clock precisely, opening hour, I had watched the face turn itself inside out and dolls in souvenir-stall national dress dance out from behind each digit to the accompaniment of 'It's a Small World After All'.

Akimi said, only a touch too well rehearsed, that was how she liked to think of the stores: a Small World of their own. They even had their own bus station.

If we had something that size at home, I said, they would probably have their own member of parliament.

'Really?' She appeared to approve.

'No. It's just we have so many MPs and MLAs – that's the sort of local MPs – and ...' She was still watching me expectantly. 'Well, what I mean is, they are *very* big.'

There was a bag I had had my eye on in Aq'a that I thought my wife would like. Might like. Though whether she liked it or not, I could just hear her now when she unwrapped it: 'A bag? I wonder where you could have got that idea?'

Bags being why I was here.

Bags being more or less all I had talked about for the last five years.

U-bags.

A revolution is afoot in food wraps. (My wife has heard it so often she could tell you it herself.) Second-stage revolution. Clingfilm – plasticised PVC, electrically charged by the act of unrolling, which thirty years ago transformed the food world, raising standards of preservation and hygiene – clingfilm will soon be consigned to the pedal bin of history.

In Brazil they have been developing an edible film made of amaranth flour. In the United States, they have been experimenting with fruits and vegetable oil. At the Dargan Industrial Park in north Belfast, after one unfortunate false start, we have made a double breakthrough. Using guaranteed one-hundred-per-cent recycled materials, we have pioneered a film that functions as a self-sealing bag. The U-bag. The principle couldn't be simpler: I mean, I tell my clients, *I* understand it. A patented dispenser concentrates the electrical charge on the edges of the film, allowing you to make up a bag on your own countertop to your own specifications, absolutely airtight. You could carry a U-bag of soup in your pocket from breakfast to lunchtime, if you were so inclined, and not spill a drop. You could carry pretty much whatever you wanted.

Our first run of ads showed a pumpkin and a pea. Orange and green. (Start local, was our motto, go global.)

'From pea purée to pumpkin pie. You choose U-bag.'

I was told it took the art director a week to find the right pea. Hundreds and hundreds he auditioned; but then that's what you pay these agencies top money for. The 'pedal bin of history', that was theirs too, as was the new company logo, a Dunlop tyre U-bagged: 'The best thing out of Belfast since the wheel.'

Now *there* was a conversation starter abroad. 'John Boyd Dunlop? Had his workshop on May Street, right round the corner from our City Hall. You didn't know?'

What the world didn't know about Belfast, frankly, could fill a book, though not the sort you were likely to find at a Writing Out of Conflict conference.

We would adapt for the Japanese market, of course. It was an art director's dream, the Japanese market. (And a sales director's: this was a country where you could buy an individual carrot shrink-wrapped.) Where would you start, or leave off, with roe? The Sogo food hall had counter after counter of the stuff, from pale pink heaps, barely solid, to great livid ox-tongues. And as for the tofu ... How long have you got?

It was to the food hall I made my footsore way now before going to find the handbag for my wife. Breakfast felt like very little and very long ago. (*Why* did I opt for fruit salad again?)

There were lunch counters around the rim of the hall, a couple more dead centre, at the bottom of the escalator from the ground floor. I chose a counter beside a stall called Sakana Zen.

(I contemplated the pairing of 'fish' and 'enlightenment' in this way, but was thrown off by the chart showing twelve species of whale, a cartoon cousin beside them in a chef's hat and apron, shouting a happy 'Let's Cook!')

My menu was a picture board suspended at eye level at the back of the counter. I plumped for picture number two: mori soba, plain noodles served cold on a bamboo platter with soy and wasabi. And since it was the lunchtime of my last day, and since I had walked all that way, and since I had been told from day one that it was the essential accompaniment, I pointed to the last picture too: a small flask of sake.

Spot hit.

Most definitely.

I raised a silent toast to myself. Apart from the mayor's office, it really hadn't been a bad week. I was close to reaching agreement with the Chamber of Commerce to include U-bagged Kleenex in November's conference welcome packs. That alone would have justified the trip, the more so as the idea only occurred to me while I was here, walking through the Hondori shopping arcade and having Kleenex packs pressed upon me at every turn. The tissues themselves were next to useless: padding for bags printed with the name of some phone company or other. The beauty of it from our point of view was that the advert was the product: the medium was the message.

A father and son sat across from me, in matching white and red Hiroshima Carp baseball jackets, silently working their way through their own platters of noodles. The boy was maybe eleven. His cheeks might have been rouged. Something in the way his diaphragm moved between swallows, I got the impression that he was asthmatic. I got the impression that he felt he fell short of his father's hopes for him.

The elderly woman next to me left, a younger woman took her place. She wore the white mask of the hay-fever sufferer and was talking through it on her mobile phone. She listened a moment, the mask creasing as though in a smile, then got up again before she had placed her order, before I could discover whether the mask was capable of eating as well as expressing emotion.

When I had finished my noodles a pot was placed before me with the water they had been cooked in. I mixed it, following the lead of the other diners, in a cup with the remains of the soy and wasabi and drank it down. The father and son had ordered seconds, so I did too. I declined the offer of more sake. I still had better than a glass left. I strained a mouthful through my teeth, trying to get to the root of the taste. Out in the food hall, Hiroshima office workers trawled the stalls for fish in all its varieties and disguises: sliced, minced, pickled, dried, soy-soaked; headless, bodiless, hollowed out, flayed; on rice, on rolls, in batter, in breadcrumbs, in their shells and out; in the case of one transparent sprick of a thing, still in seawater, still living. I couldn't swear to it, my Japanese being better on the page than on the ear, but I even thought I could hear 'sakana' in the song being piped around the basement.

The father and son in the Carp jackets left. I finished the second platter of noodles, drank the cooking water and then the last of the sake.

Now that there was a bit of distance between them and me, I found myself smiling at the events of the morning. It would be something to tell people when I got home, that was for sure. Your man leaning forward in the car, banging on about New York in the fall. And what was it he had said about speaking English and driving? 'There's a few' – no, 'plenty' – 'plenty at home have trouble with it.'

He could be amusing enough when he wasn't too far up himself. And he was there on Amazon: you could add him to your wish-list, order him with a single click.

I took the escalator from the food hall, got on another one that I remembered, too late, went straight from second floor to fourth. Third, I wanted. I wandered around till I found the way back down, followed the signs for Aq'a, then lost them, then picked them up again. I stopped a few times, lifted things, last-minute souvenir things, did a quick price conversion, set them down.

The passageway came upon me quite unexpectedly. Halfway along it I began to suspect I had gone wrong again: the noise, partly, the sudden outdoorsy smell. (Outdoors? Up here?) I walked on, turned left, tripped down a few steps, and found myself in a large, tiled hall that on first glance resembled a covered market – fast-food stalls rubbing shoulders with racks of garish blouses, comic-book spinners hard by fridges full of beer. Then a bus passed before the doors at the far end (an equal distance behind me, people were looking at themselves anxiously in mirrors on the third floor of a department store) and in that instant the hall revealed its true nature. Now it was the ticket machines that caught my eye, the timetables, high up, in orange, white and blue. Akimi, on the first day, had omitted to mention that the bus station was not, in fact, at ground level.

I walked past the food stalls, clothes racks, book spinners and fridges and out through the doors as another bus pulled in at a platform, 'Hiroshima University' in a panel on its side.

Maybe it was the sake, maybe it was the jibe earlier outside the café, but I decided then and there I would get on it. Twenty minutes, Kimiko had said. Call it half an hour by bus. It was still only lunchtime. I could be out there and back well before four. It wouldn't even matter if I didn't see him. I could leave him a note – on the back of the bus ticket, if it was big enough. 'Was just passing …'

I boarded. The bus driver wore white gloves and a squashed peaked cap.

'University?' I asked, double-checking. He looked at me; shook his head.

'*Iie?*' I said. It was difficult to be confident in a language where 'no' sounded like a casual 'yes'.

The driver waved a white-gloved hand at me: stand aside. A queue was building at my back. I offered him the smallest note I had, five thousand yen. He waved it away, and the change pocket that I then opened to him. I stepped down off the bus, looked at the side panel. There it was, 'Hiroshima University'. Even the Japanese characters looked familiar from my two-week Kanji crash course in the early new year: 'big', and 'child' with a three-pronged crown, meaning 'school'.

I watched the people in the queue, what they did when they boarded the bus, pulling tickets from a machine on the right just inside the doors. I fell in behind them and pulled a ticket too, a white square with a faint purplish number one. The driver made a point of not looking at me as I passed.

I found a seat a third the way down. It was better upholstered than a bus seat at home, but there was something dingy about the bus itself. Dingy and troublingly diesel-smelling. 'Deregulated' was the word that sprang to mind. Whoever had peddled the stereotype of Japanese hyper-efficiency in all things motorised had never got on a bus in the Sogo bus centre, any more than the person who had peddled the one about industrial design had experienced the Three-Day-Week chic of the Hiroshima JETRO office.

There was a display above the windscreen: numbers one to twenty; two hundred yen below the one; blanks below the rest. All in all it had the air of a mobile bingo parlour.

The studenty-looking woman across the aisle was watching me from beneath lime green eyeshadow.

'Speak English?' I asked, then, getting a nod, 'University?' Treble-check. She nodded again and looked down at her book. I relaxed.

The engine started at the second attempt. The bus juddered through a one-hundred-and-eighty-degree turn then began to pick up speed on the three-storey slip road, so that at the bottom it shot across four lanes of traffic, as though carried by the momentum alone and never mind the green light in its favour; across four lanes and up the side of Hiroshima Castle. (Was taken there day two of my stay. Nothing to write home about, I wrote home.) On the opposite side, the left, was a park, or perhaps just a tree-lined parking lot, with stalls set up under awnings, a sharp contrast to the blocks of flats – not apartment blocks: flats – which immediately after filled the bus windows, close to the road. Then the landscape changed again, the flats giving way to older, single-family homes. What's this they called the style in the States? Not wood-frame. *Clapboard.*

I remembered, with a faint prick of shame, what Ike had said about the Midwest. The roadside neon was all fast food and diners: McDonald's, Mister Donut, Sunday's Sun, Jolly Pasta. For a time we were travelling beneath an elevated railway, running right up the middle of the street. I craned my neck to read the signs above the road: Miyoshi/Kabe, Oshiba Water Gate East.

We had been driving for a quarter of an hour when we crossed one of the rivers, wide and shallow-looking at this point, broken by islands of scrub. It was when we picked up a sign for the airport (40 km) ten minutes later, having joined a fully-fledged motorway in the meantime, that I began to wonder. Where was the tunnel Tadao had pointed out to me from Mount Ogon-zan? And if the airport was forty kilometres off, what did it signify that the university wasn't even being mentioned yet?

I gave it a couple of minutes more then leaned into the aisle. 'Excuse me,' I said and the woman with the green eyeshadow looked up from her book. 'How much longer to the university?'

She consulted her watch. It was like something a child would have, bright pink strap, kitten on the face. 'Forty-five minutes?' she said.

I laughed. 'No, I think there must be a mistake. *Forty*-five? That's three-quarters of an hour.'

She moved her head, caught between a nod and a shake. 'Yes, I know. That is how long it always takes.'

'But I was told it was only twenty minutes by car.'

'Ah!' Her face cleared. 'You mean *that* university.'

Past her head all I could see was motorway and mountain. 'That university?'

'Hiroshima City.'

Of course, it was *hyaku man toshi*. Why would it not have more than one?

I flopped back in my seat. I would just have to sit tight and pay a double fare. There were figures now, too, on the display below numbers two to seven, corresponding to the stops we had made to take on passengers. The figure below number one now read six hundred yen. It was like a taxi clock.

'Sorry.' The woman was leaning towards me. 'You want to go back to city soon?'

I got the feeling that she was keeping the English simple for my benefit.

'Yes.'

'I don't think this bus will go back.'

I must have looked horrified.

'Don't worry,' she said. 'In a few minutes there is a stop. I will show you. You can cross over.'

'And can you tell me which bus to look out for?'

'Oh' – she was trying not to smile – 'there is only one.'

I sat on the edge of my seat while she kept watch for me. It was closer to five minutes and the motorway had reverted to two-lane mountain road when she suddenly pointed out the right-hand side. 'There.'

A vending machine. A bench. A Perspex shelter.

I was straight up on to my feet. 'Thank you. Thank you.'

The driver's eyes looked at me, alarmed, in the rear-view mirror as I staggered towards the front. He began shouting.

'It's OK.' I wedged myself against a seat and fumbled in my pocket for my wallet. 'I have it exactly.'

He shouted louder. He looked as though, if he hadn't had a couple of tons of bus to control, he would have taken his white-gloved hands from the wheel and throttled me.

'He is saying you have to sit down,' my helpful neighbour called to me.

I sat and twenty yards on the bus stopped.

I gave the driver my ticket and my yen. He shook his head as he dropped them, where I should evidently have dropped them, into the metal chute of the contraption attached to his cab's half-door. He pressed a button. The main doors opened with a pneumatic *pish*.

'*Domo*' – I climbed down and the doors closed again behind me – '*arigato*.' Thanks a bunch.

The bus went round a corner and out of sight. I walked across the empty road and down the hill to the bus shelter. About a mile farther down was a filling station with a yard full of cars out back. Behind the bus shelter the road fell away to a pond, maybe fifty yards across, with a stand of dark-coloured trees at the far end and a crane, looking a little typecast and more than a little forlorn, in the middle. (Did it occur to me to question the day's bounty of birds? In a word, no. From my conservatory at home I could spot half a dozen species whose like I wouldn't expect to find in Japan. Smaller than an eagle, admittedly. Less statuesque than a crane.) The wind blew. The crane's feathers ruffled. I looked at the timetable. Sure enough, it consisted of a single column. One bus, once an hour. I checked my watch. I had missed the last one by ten minutes. I sat on the bench.

Across from me, and set back from the road, was a pair of houses, windows shuttered beneath roofs of matching glazed blue tiles. I wasn't a hundred per cent sure there was no one inside, but I was certain I did not want to go knocking to find out. A broad, dirt track curved behind them and over a ridge. I coughed just to hear myself cough. At the end of a silent minute more, a lorry appeared on the ridge, laden with stone, and started down the track slowly enough that I was able to change my mind five or six times about asking the driver for a lift as far as the filling station – further if he was going. I had just settled on 'yes', ask, had my feet planted firmly on the ground ready to stand, when the lorry at last came round the bend on to the road and the driver smiled at me. No: *smirked.*

It was the strangest thing. He seemed entirely unsurprised to see me. When he winked I was right back in Tadao's car, driving past the Ogon-zan road works. I slipped my hand into my pocket and closed it round my phone. Even if I couldn't dial it blind, it would at least add heft to my fist.

As soon as the lorry was gone I realised I was being ridiculous. The driver had had plenty of time to observe me as he drove down the track. I could not have looked anything but lost. He might even have guessed my mistake exactly. 'Wrong university! Stupid bloody foreigner.' And I was at the bus stop. It wasn't like I couldn't get back to the city eventually, or walk the mile to the filling station, for that matter.

I walked the fraction of it to the vending machine and put in two hundred yen for a bottle of water – I could drink it as I walked the rest of the way – only to discover when I took off the lid it wasn't water at all, but something transparent and syrupy.

Which was when the cloud appeared, travelling low, fast, and dark from the direction that the bus had been headed. The wind went up a notch beneath it; the crane's feathers went from ruffled to buffeted. It spread its wings, hoisted its ridiculous legs out of the water and set them down again in the shelter of the trees. The rain came in huge splodges. I pulled my jacket around me and ran for cover myself, cursing Ike for goading me, the heavens for opening on me, but most of all – sitting now, watching the rain turn to hail – cursing my own stupidity. I shouldn't have been here. Really. Not within a thousand miles.

2

The morning after my first visit to the A-Bomb Museum with Haraguchi-san I decided to return alone, do it the justice of solemn – and, if I wanted it, silent – contemplation. I almost turned back at the door. The foyer was heaving. Three coach-loads of primary-school children were being ushered in ahead of me, boisterousness barely held in check. An attendant beckoned me in another door, fast track for small groups and singles. Well, even with the hire of the headset you were only talking a couple of quid. If it all got too much I could press on through and out the other end, no harm done. I went in.

I was on the ground floor, just past the display case with the watch stopped for ever at eight-fifteen, dividing the museum into unequal parts, before and after, city and symbol, when a woman, turning suddenly from another display, almost collided with me. We made brief eye contact; smiled. I took a few steps to the left, to the circular scale model – itself the diameter of a landmine crater – of the city in the aftermath of the bomb: the original ground zero, a brown waste broken only by the red marker indicating the hyper centre, three-hundred scale-metres adrift of Aioi Bridge, and the handful of buildings, ferro-concrete like the Dome, which had withstood the blast.

One of these, the Bank of Japan on Rijo-dori, famously opened for business on 8 August 1945, the same day that the trams began running again. The building was there still, some kind of gallery now, round the corner from my hotel. I had wandered in one afternoon in the middle of an architecture degree show. Future cities in polystyrene and balsa wood, minutely populated with pedestrians and diners and couples in clinches and even a jazz band on a rooftop, trumpets raised to the sky.

The longer I stared into the crater the bleaker the memory of those models became. A huff and a puff and all the houses that ever were, or ever would be, were history.

As I turned I caught the woman's eye again. She had been reading the reasons why Hiroshima was targeted: military bases, few allied prisoners, no previous air raids to mask the impact of the A-bomb. Our smiles, this time, were of a double recognition, 'us again' tempered by 'all this'.

She was dark-haired, broad-shouldered in her vest top, a year or two either side of thirty, at a guess. Her guide-book was in Spanish, though I would have had her as coming from somewhere much closer to this part of the world.

Such was the press of people, the tendency for clusters to form around exhibits, it was hard to tell if she was on her own or with a tour party. We moved apart again. I was pulled up by the life-sized reproduction of a photograph – one of only five the photographer could bear to take that day – of victims sitting by a riverside wall, hugging their knees, too weak to flee the whirlwind headed their way; then was borne along by the crowd up the stairs to the next, mezzanine, level. The establishment of the Atomic Bomb Casualty Commission. The complaint of victims: 'They examine us, but don't treat us.' The uncomfortably familiar-sounding story of the Hiroshima Maidens, twenty-five young women with terrible scarring on their faces and arms, flown to the US for surgery in a flurry of tabloid headlines in the early summer of 1955. They ruin us then feel good for treating us.

On an impulse I walked to the railing overlooking the ground floor. The woman – I had no trouble picking her out – wasn't on her own, nor was she with a party, but was resting one hand on the shoulder of a preppily dressed Chinese guy, who was now studying the guide-book, while she, half a pace behind, directed a puzzled gaze at me. I recoiled, caught out. *What was I thinking?* She was with her husband or boyfriend. She was a good dozen years younger than me, striking-looking, the more I saw her. We weren't in a film where striking-looking women casually hit on strangers a dozen or more years their seniors. (My in-flight movie en route to Tokyo was *Lost in Translation*. I mean, come on.) We were in the Hiroshima A-Bomb Museum, for God's sake, in the midst of heartbreak and horror.

Running was hardly an option. Still, I did the closest thing to it, putting my head down and jinking through the crowd, up more stairs, before the woman would arrive on the mezzanine. I was tempted to skip the next room entirely (the nuclear arms race: I had spent a long time here listening to Haraguchi-san read figures off the wall), but it was impossible to pass through any part of the museum without your conscience or compassion snagging on something.

I had missed the dog the day before. It was only a bit-part player in a longer video loop, looking like any old mutt tethered to a post any old where, until a split second later (a split second of mind-bending physics later) that spot became precisely the worst place on earth. The dog leapt and twisted in the nuclear-test wind. If it could have reached the lead it would have bitten through it. If it could have reached its own neck it would have bitten through that.

The woman passed within inches of my nose as I wheeled around from the screen, her face drained of expression. In my confusion I started back the other way, against the tide, and there was the guy, coming straight for me, guide-book cleaving the air between us. I opened my mouth: I could explain; but – '*Excusa, excusa!*' – he too pushed past. I began to think that the woman couldn't have seen me, and hard on the heels of this came another thought: she hadn't seen me even though she was in fact looking for me. I felt a fizz between my ribs.

No. Impossible.

I did an about-face, prepared to follow the recommended route, but, slow, I told myself. *Slow.*

A primary-school group had gathered with their teacher before the account of the memorial mound, which, somewhere out there in the Peace Park, contained the ashes of seventy-thousand victims of the bomb. It was hard to tell, looking at the children, whether the teacher's words meant any more to them than they did to me with my single fingernail's grasp of Japanese. Seventy thousand dead in a flash, it was so beyond most eight-year-olds' imagining as to be nonsensical even in their own tongue.

I left as the teacher began giving her charges a pep talk (or so I interpreted it from her expression) for the rooms ahead. The rooms ahead were so dreadful that even Haraguchi-san had been lost for words. Here were the testimonies of survivors, the personal effects of those they loved who had died: shredded clothes; a piano harmonica; a belt; a lunchbox with its never-to-be-eaten lunch; a wooden sandal, the print of the foot still inside; a tricycle; another, less famous watch, stopped at eight-fifteen (who had directed 'this one downstairs, that one up'?); a human shadow burnt on to stone steps; fragments of a child's skin and nails, hoarded by a mother to show her husband, still overseas; the unidentified bone fragments taken home by another father and treated as though they were his own lost daughter's.

I found the woman on a bench before a video screen in a room off a corridor whose final exhibit was a heap of rubble with items to which no stories attached: golf clubs, bottles, a pair of leather boots, insulating tubes, an ashtray, coins fused together, a portable safe, a clock with a melted glass face; and statues, of the birth of Buddha, of Daikokuten, God of Wealth, of Bishamonten, God of Treasure, of Kannon, Goddess of Mercy, missing both her arms.

The voice in my headset had transformed itself into a soft moan. A teenage girl searching with her father in the ruins of her home.

Ah!
I find Mother's bones.
Ah! I hold them close.
A white powder stirred by the breeze.
I put Mother's bone in my mouth.
It tastes sad.
An unbearable sadness overwhelms us.
Wailing
we pick up the bones together.
The bones make a rustling sound in the candy box.

The woman looked up as I entered, her own headset pushed down round her neck, as though she couldn't take one word more. There was a space on the bench beside her and for a moment I thought I would not be able to resist sitting down, putting my arms around her. I urged myself instead to the furthest end of the room and to what I remembered from the previous day to be the strangest exhibit of all. In a glass case hung a mahogany frame, maybe thirty-six inches by thirty, containing roughly seven and a half square feet of plaster etched with vertical lines, faint on the left, darker towards the midpoint, more concentrated (a seismographic reading, I had thought, or a howl, petrified), faltering then, running off true, finally fading altogether.

Black-rain stains.

This was before I had stumbled upon the basement and the sky of flames. I would never have believed then that anything man-made could have made the terror of that time more real.

The man beside me moved away and another stepped in to take his place. It was the shirtsleeve I noticed first, pink, Brooks Brothers, cuffing a wrist, at the end of which dangled a Spanish guide-book. My heart quickened. He turned a page of the book. The band on the wedding-ring finger looked entirely un-blemished. (Hiroshima on honeymoon?) I tried to get a fix on his face reflected in the display cabinet. Soft, that was my first thought. Not unappealing, but still – there was really no other word – soft. I had seen it on fellas I went to school with, who had seemed never to become fully adult before they started to get old.

I tried to imagine her loving that face and had to blink away the thought of her cheeks streaked black with tears of regret. I met my own gaze. Well, what would anyone make of me? What did she? Unless it was true what people said, without the suit …

I gave my diluted image the once over, gave myself the benefit of the doubt, and left him to contemplate those awful lines.

The woman was standing now, her back to her husband, at the wall devoted to Sadako Sasaki, who at the age of two had been blown ten feet across a room by the blast and who had died of leukaemia, aged twelve, despite exceeding the thousand origami cranes she had convinced herself would save her life. I knew from yesterday, we were approaching the end.

I fell in at the back of the line moving silently, erratically, along the bare dozen yards of Sadako's life, letting myself be carried to within feet of the woman as one by one the people ahead of me stepped around her. When at last no one remained to separate us I slowed to her almost imperceptible leftwards drift. Again, fragments were all I could get side-on: a mole high up on her bare brown arm; a two-inch stretch of pink satin beneath the cotton of a vest strap; the tip of her nose; the twinned rings, once, when she moved her hand. I had no idea if she was conscious of me. I couldn't look at her face in the glass for fear of finding myself transfixed. I concentrated on Sadako's cranes, getting smaller and smaller the further she had gone beyond the thousandth, using a pin to help her fold them, as though she had set herself a new target, an atom-sized crane, split along the back into two microscopic wings, unleashing who knows what healing power.

All that remained of the attempt were the handful of carefully cut squares of cellophane – actual paper still being scarce – that she had not got round to folding when she died.

How long I had been staring at these, or what exactly was going through my mind, I cannot say, though Tom and Jill were mixed in there, Tom and Jill as they were when their need of me was not weighed in pounds sterling. All the alarms of their growing run together.

I felt a sudden, choking sense of grief and loss: had actually to put my hand to my throat to check the swallow.

Only then did I realise the woman was not beside me.

I looked at the space where she had been. I looked over my shoulder at the black rain. I looked at all the points in between, but saw no sign of her or her husband. Another corridor opened beyond Sadako's wall. I turned the corner into it quicker than I knew was decent, and stopped.

There, at the far end of the corridor, she stood, facing me, before a picture of the first flowers to bloom on the scorched plain, and next to an arrow pointing right, to the exit. My haste must have been unmistakable, but she didn't so much as blink. We were about ten feet apart, not close enough that I ought to have been able to see what I would swear I did see, the pulse of a million simultaneous calculations on the rims of her eyes. Yet her smile was immediate, without restraint. She was not striking. She was beautiful. I answered with a smile of my own, not quite as certain. I knew that in such circumstances seconds were all you had to decide. The next thing was to speak – *no hablo español* – to ask her name, where she was staying, what we were going to do about this. But her husband … I had no way of telling where he was: round the next corner, for all I knew, practically at her back.

I allowed my head to droop a fraction and, still smiling, shook it, once: a reminder to myself, *this was not a film.* She lurched forward from the shoulders, pulled herself in again, her expression changing in an instant from disbelief to something like disdain. A German couple passed, either side of me, their leggy, pre-teen sons trailing behind, looking from me to the woman and back. The woman turned on her heel, started walking. I followed, the German family in between.

The only person round the corner was the attendant collecting the headsets. I watched the woman as she surrendered hers, balancing the strap on the tip of one straining finger, trying to make light of it, and I knew she had gambled back there in the corridor. There was one more right-pointing arrow. She obeyed it without a backward glance.

Her husband was turning circles by the exit, fifty yards away. She raised her hand as she walked towards him. His went up almost involuntarily in reply. He recomposed his face, making light of his own strain. The German boys looked back at me.

'What?' I mouthed.

I spotted her in the park a short time later, not far from the queue for the Peace Bell, skipping as she talked to her husband, making grabs for his hand, stamping her foot at a persistent pigeon. You observed it in everyone, of course, the relief at being outside again in the spring sunshine, free from the bone dust. Hers, though, was relief of a different order. She had let herself walk right to edge of a precipice and had had a good look at what lay below. I think she knew she could, at the time of her choosing, take the next step and live. She was relieved, but excited. Her husband, by the looks of him, could not quite believe his luck, to have landed her in the first place, to have her dancing around him like this.

I last saw them, arm in arm, on the Dome side of the bridge below Aioi, headed past the spot indicated in the museum by the red marker, towards the Hondori Arcade. I sat on a seat on the Peace Park side. A small pleasure boat passed between us, turning in a wide arc beneath the short stem of the Aioi Bridge's T, a scurf of cherry blossom washed by the wake against the wall below me. Behind me, the Peace Bell tolled and a few seconds later tolled again.

Oh, God. What had I done? *Not* done. Not said. A single word would have been enough. She would have taken the step. It didn't matter that she might never have looked at me twice had she met me outside. Normal rules did not apply in there. The whole place was a monument to the unprecedented.

The day before, I had paused on my way out to read the visitors' book. 'A terrible reminder,' someone had written. It was terrible: how destructive the weapons were; how quickly lives could be extinguished, or turned inside out; how short a time, really, when you thought about it, any of us had here.

Why not gamble?

3

A truck rumbled by, coming from the ridge above the shuttered houses.

The rain had stopped. The cloud that had brought it was now beyond the filling station and its back-lot of new-rinsed cars, and headed for the city. I looked over my shoulder. The crane was back where I had first seen it, in the middle of the pond. It occurred to me that it might be waiting for something too. A fish to move, another crane to happen by.

The phone rang in my pocket. I tugged it out.

'So, did you get yourself lost?' he said.

'What?' I stood up and peered out of the bus shelter. The road was empty right and left; the houses opposite were as impenetrable as ever.

'I was worried about you walking off into town like that.'

I sat down again. 'Thanks, but I'm fine.'

There was a lot of noise behind him, voices in competition

with crockery. Coffee break?

'After all,' he said, 'you have a story belonging to me.'

Someone standing close to him laughed, the Croatian national hero perhaps.

'Yeah, yeah, yeah,' I said. The laughter drifted out of range, may not, after all, have been connected.

'And I was going to invite you to a reception tonight. End of conference. If you've all your shopping done in time.'

'Of course I'll have it done,' I said, too quickly. 'I've had the whole afternoon.'

'Well, then.'

'I'll think about it.' Why was he being so friendly? Why was I being so grudging? 'Thanks. That might be nice.'

'Drinks at six. It will be well signposted. The shell and the pen. Oh, and you know, don't you, there's more than one university? Make sure when you get the taxi …'

'Hiroshima City,' I said. 'I know, I know.'

The bus arrived forty minutes later. I had made myself pretty comfortable in the meantime, legs crossed on the bench, Paul Smith jacket pillowed behind my neck. And since the water was actually syrup and since – well, I was halfway up a mountain, what other excuse did I need? – I had bought a beer from the vending machine. When was the last time I had done that? Sat outside in the afternoon drinking beer?

I was nearly sorry, when the bus finally pulled away, to be leaving. I dipped my head as I walked down the aisle, hoping for one last glimpse of the crane. It was pecking at something under its wing, as though to emphasise that my coming or going was a matter of the utmost indifference. It raised its bill and a shudder ran the length of its neck, then it was lost to me.

The bus was less ramshackle than the one that had brought me up. There was carpet on the floor, a white slipcover on my headrest. I noticed that several of the passengers had reclined their seats and fallen asleep. I searched for the button and eased my own seat back. Music leaked, almost familiar, from a young lad's earphones directly in front of me. I watched the filling station pass, coming out of my recline briefly as I realised the cars I had seen gleaming out the back were all scrap; watched the mountain road rejoin the motorway, the overhead signs telling me that all this time I had been only ten miles from the city.

I closed my eyes, replaying on my internal screen a television programme I had chanced upon on my first night in Tokyo, jet-lagged and unable to sleep: an update on a documentary made in the sixties, or so I guessed from the black-and-white footage interspersed throughout. The subjects were a couple living on a farm in the mountains somewhere outside Tokyo. In the earlier film the man had gone off at the start of each week to work on the city's building sites, his face against the window of the early morning train a picture of misery. At work, he ran everywhere. Even with a wheelbarrow full of bricks he ran, even pushing the barrow up an angled plank, as though he could get the week over and done with faster that way.

In the update he was housebound, virtually immobile. All that time finally run down. The woman, small and pretty before, was so old she was bent double, leaning on a mattock for support outdoors. Indoors, her gait was almost ape-like, reliant on her hands for power and balance. She touched every inch of the house as she moved through it, as if they had grown to be a perfect fit for one another. The less her husband stirred abroad the more she was obliged to. She cut the grass with a hand scythe. She harvested soya beans and soaked them in the stream that ran past the farmhouse, then she mashed a batch in boiling water and strained the milk for tofu. Other beans she mixed with rice and placed in a vat to make miso.

At some stage in the filming the man died. The commentary must have explained this, but the first I knew of it was the woman cutting two slices of tofu and placing them before his picture on the household shrine. She covered her face with her hands for a long time. She went back into the fields. She scythed the grass and tried to push the laden wheelbarrow. Three paces, stop; three paces, stop ...

Her knees were so swollen she had difficulty rolling her trousers past them. At night she placed lit cigarette butts in tiny metal holders on the swelling. (There was no visual clue to where the butts came from, unless her husband had hoarded them against such a day all those years ago on the building sites of Tokyo.) She lay on a mat before her husband's shrine, sobbing.

At the end, the camera pulled back off her, bent over her work, into an aerial shot: a wooden building on a mountainside, a stream, seven irregularly shaped fields, maybe an acre in total. A universe.

I opened my eyes as the bus arrived at the stand in the Sogo bus centre. The young lad in front of me with the head full of music got to his feet, spilling another nearly recognisable drop of it. I checked the fare against the number on my ticket and with a veteran's casualness deposited them both in the machine. The driver thanked me and I told him in my best Japanese he was welcome.

A door marked Aq'a led off the platform and up a short flight of steps into the very calm third floor of the department store. All that was missing was the actress playing my wife stepping forward to tell me that the entire bus episode had been another bad dream.

I took a couple of further wrong turns, trying to find the outlet where I had seen the handbag I was after. At one point I wound up back in the Sogo food hall. The fish song was playing again. Though it was tipping into late afternoon, the lunch counters were still full. I wouldn't have needed much persuasion now myself to have another bite. Another sake.

Later. Sooner rather than.

The bag was all that I remembered it to be, and more to the point, unlike anything I could remember seeing in Belfast. As

I was waiting for it to be wrapped I went back to the display stand and picked up a purse: same designer, different style. I asked the assistant to wrap it separately, then, when she was just about to tie the ribbon, to unwrap it for a second. I put in a hundred yen coin.

For luck. For Norma.

I had had an awful premonition about Norma and me, the morning of my third visit to the A-Bomb Museum. I had turned up at its doors twenty-four hours to the minute after I had last walked through them, having persuaded myself that in this place of stopped watches I might be offered some way to retrieve the moment, repair the past. If I was that woman, I thought, I would come back at this time too.

As I walked across the bridge from my hotel it really didn't seem such a long shot. The coaches disgorging their passengers – primary-school parties, teenage American tourists, Korean pensioners – looked no different to the previous day's coaches. The taxi drivers stood by the doors of their cabs, smoking, laughing into their chests, as though engaged in the same gruffly humorous conversation as before.

I knew, though, the second I was inside, that she wouldn't show, that my being there was a hundred kinds of wrong. And yet I couldn't drag myself away. Another minute, I bargained with myself, and inwardly counted it off. Another minute more.

I had a lunchtime meeting, rearranged from the day before when I had phoned to say I was feeling a bit under the weather. (*Crushed*, I could have said.) I might have stood in the foyer till then had it not been for my bladder – too embarrassingly full all of a sudden for a toilet with a woman cleaner wandering around in it – and for the sky of flames, which evaporated even its urgings.

As it was, I sat for maybe twenty minutes more in the basement, staring into the *Holocaust*, feeling myself reduced to something like my essence. Not a sales executive, not a father, not a husband, or even a name. The person a stranger smiled at in an empty corridor. The person who left his hotel room this morning fully prepared never to return, but who would now have to climb the stairs and walk out the doors and back into it all: home, family, work …

Nothing good would come of Norma and me, I saw that. Nothing good for her more than for me: emails, lunches, meaningful looks, a single moment of madness somewhere down the line; weeks, stretching into months, of regret. Not a step off the precipice, just one of those little falls to which a marriage is prone, for which children and a comfortable home provide such an effective safety net. She would knock at my door one day, stand with her back to it when called to come in (she would have had something interesting done with her hair, a streak, an asymmetric fringe), tell me she didn't think in the circumstances she could go on working here. And I would tell her that I wished she would reconsider, that I would be sorry – careful how I said it – to lose her.

'I know,' she would say, finding a smile despite everything. 'I know.'

I saw it all.

Something else I saw that morning, which I had missed on both my previous visits to the museum: the gigantic ceremonial drum, resting on a carved turtle's back, at the far end of the foyer, beyond the pay-desk. In commemoration of the sister agreement between Hiroshima and the Korean city of Taegu. Artist Kim Jong Moon, Taegu Intangible Cultural Asset Number 12.

Ike was here, at least once.

I strolled back to the hotel with my presents, the route taking me one last time along a stretch of Hondori Arcade, which ran from close to the Peace Park in the east, to the Parco department store, three-quarters of a mile to the west. Today, as every day, it was teeming with shoppers. Today, as every day, the din beneath its high arched roof was tremendous. (To look up at the ribs of that roof was to see the whale from the plankton's point of view.) Most of the shops had open frontage on to the street. More than a few had someone posted on the threshold, stuffing packs of Kleenex into your fist, or simply hollering their wares. Music came from every side, and from every one of the last five decades, and all was beaten into a cocked hat by the innocuous-looking beat-box on a table before a chemist's shop that played nothing else but Wham!, little else but 'Bad Boys'.

I turned down a side street inhabited, at its lower end, almost entirely by shoe shops. The stock in each was almost identical. The hollerers hollered twice as hard. At the upper end, outside a convenience store whose Hiroshima area manager I had met on my second day in the city, there were Hanami mats for sale, plastic affairs in off-licence blue: a few cheap square feet between you and the guys drinking Special Brew in Belfast parks; a few cheap square feet that might have been a world.

As I came out on to the boulevard just below the hotel, I caught a glimpse of a monk's red robe and bowed head moving erratically through the suits and T-shirts and dresses of the pedestrians to my left. There was a shrine around here, I remembered, which I had taken some photographs of, but no sooner had I thought this than I thought *white* robes in Japan, and I turned to see not a monk at prayer come abreast of me, but a barefoot tramp, head bent over a transistor radio; not a robe, but a blanket, tied at the waist with a rope from which toy robots and dolls and cowbells hung.

I pulled money from my pocket. What with the shopping bags, the movement was more awkward and finally more sudden than I had intended. The tramp glanced up at me as though I was about to strike him.

'No.' I said, '*Iie.*' But he backed away, shaking his head. A Snoopy swung below his navel, exaggerating the gesture. A woman, passing in the same direction, carrying a black dog not much bigger than the Snoopy, looked over her shoulder at me, as if to say I ought to be ashamed.

'All right.' I put the money back in my pocket. I wasn't going to pursue this. 'All right.'

With a clatter of robots and bells, the tramp shuffled off. I shivered. The sun had lost none of its shine but a little of its heat after the shower. I avoided the shadows of the ornamental gardens on the road up to the hotel, then stopped, inside the door.

Change for the Better, I thought, or rather saw: the little charity envelope in the net on the seatback on the aeroplane here. And the coins the tramp had refused didn't feel quite as heavy in my pocket as I crossed the lobby to the lifts.

reception

.

1

There were two emails waiting for me on the laptop, one inevitably from Norma, on the office account. Seven fifty-nine. *You know me, I like to get in before the rush.* I knew that for half an hour some mornings we were practically the only ones in the building. I scanned the rest of the email quickly: was I going to the brand protection conference in London? Would I be interested in next year's Asia Packaging Exhibition in Osaka? Could I be tempted to write a short report for the Invest Japan newsletter? Nothing now, thank goodness, about Sardinia – that was past. Nothing, in fact, that couldn't keep till I got home. I hit reply. *Deal with all this Monday. See you then, bright-eyed and bushy-tailed.*

Seeing how the thing was bound to turn out, clearly didn't mean I was able to stop it happening.

The other email was from Tom. Had I remembered that phone? Only, the one he had at the minute was pretty knackered, well not so knackered he hadn't already promised a mate he could have it when Tom got his new one, because the mate had his old one stolen and … and so it went on for a further five lines.

I started to email him back, standing there leaning over the keyboard while I removed my shoes and socks, using only the toes of the opposite foot, and then I thought, Look at you! You're not an online catalogue. He's not your customer. He's your son. It's a gift. Remember 'Wow Dad, thanks'? I clicked X. A box popped up. Did I want to save changes to this email? No – click – I did not. Let him sweat. It wasn't much, but it was the closest I was likely to come now with him or Jill to the genuine surprise of old.

I finished undressing, folding my clothes straight into my suitcase, then stepped into the shower again and let the water drum some of the early evening torpor out of me. There went the double portion of lunchtime noodles; there went the sake, the can of beer. The grit that swirled around my feet was nothing ordinary. You would have thought I had been roaming the hills for a week, rather than sitting for an hour on a bench. I wondered did it work the other way round, were there flecks of me in the dust of the bus shelter, getting under the crane's feathers? I squeezed my eyes tight shut, bleaching out the image, and raised my face to the spray. For a time, thought itself was washed away. I don't remember getting out of the shower.

The screen was filled with rows of neatly stacked skulls when I switched on the TV. I stopped towelling my hair. Rwanda, Genocide Week. The news channels had been trailing it since I arrived in Japan. Twice I had woken in the wee small hours with the remote in my hand and those same empty eyes looking at me.

The skulls dissolved into rows of men in pink pyjamas staring from behind prison bars. I muted the commentary until the headlines would come on and carried on across the room, towel over my shoulder, to the window, which I opened to the full extent of the safety latch. Hiroshima poured in, going for the ears and nose.

A man stood at the rail of one of the two oyster restaurants anchored on the river to my right, smoking and talking animatedly to an unseen someone in what I took, from the man's apron, to be the kitchen. He was either very angry or very happy, shouting or laughing.

Laughing, I decided; there was too much unhappiness to add to it unnecessarily.

I padded around my room, packing as much as I could for the morning. Just in case.

I lifted the *Trade and Labelling Handbook* from my bedside table and squeezed it into my carry-on bag alongside the novel that I had last seen the night before I left home.

'I don't know why you're even bothering with that,' my wife had said. Always said.

I lifted the novel out, set it on the table. I never slept well the night before a flight, even with a couple of drinks. As an afterthought, I lifted *Trade and Labelling* out again too and laid it on top. Save the novel for the flight.

There was tennis on the TV. I'd missed the headlines. I turned up the volume and ran down the music channels for something appropriate to dressing for a last night out; I don't know – George Benson. I settled for Cameo, 'Word Up'.

'Do you dance, do your dance quick Mama …'

I did a few steps of mine over to the wardrobe (I could still surprise a few people at the Christmas party) and slid back the door. Suit, definitely: the dark grey; but not a tie. I thought of Ike and the other conference delegates I had seen floating around the hotel in the last few days. No, a tie would be much too much. I hunted in the case for the new polo shirt I had treated myself to the day before yesterday. Long-sleeved, aubergine. Not my usual suit style, but – 'no romance, no romance,' I sang as I slipped it over my head – it didn't go at all badly.

At the last minute I went back to the case for a U-bag information pack. End-of-conference receptions had to be catered too, and this was a work trip after all. The computer was still on. I sent Tom a quick email: *Don't worry*. At the door I turned around a second time and went and dug out a plain white shirt to change into. I looked in the mirror. Better. The case was a mess again. I let myself out, resigned to having to repack when I got back.

The cleaning cart was parked by the lifts in its early evening guise of drinks trolley: plastic baskets mounted fore and aft, bristling with bottles for the minibars. A clipboard rested on the foremost basket, sheets attached to it with ticks in boxes beside the drinks replaced. I flicked back four sheets to the nineteenth floor. One room had ticks against it right across the page, starting with the champagne and ending (you could just imagine them being opened in sequence) with the coffee liqueur and peach schnapps. I checked the room number. It wasn't Ike's.

The first three lifts that stopped were all packed and all going up. Even with the renovation work, the Skylight restaurant and bar were big draws at this time of year. The fourth lift – it was still awaiting its own makeover – was empty but for the smell of perfume. 'Sweet Island Mystery by Feejee Fragrance,' I said under my breath, enjoying the words, remembering the bottle on prominent display on the JETRO reception desk, a makeshift paperweight for the vinyl-covered folder beneath containing photographs of other products that had gained a toehold in the prefecture.

I gave myself twenty-two floors now to remember as many as I was able: Algerian Coffee, Bond Street truffle sauce, yoghurt incubators, dog lunchboxes, cat car-seats, transparent pool balls, Velcro draughtboards, fluorescent foam hands, fluorescent foam feet, painted cow skulls, tomahawks, a twentieth-century commemorative cup and saucer set from Glasgow: Jesse Owens, the Beatles, not a mushroom cloud in sight.

Ding. Ground floor. Didn't I do well?

The lobby, quiet when I had passed through half an hour before, was jammed: non-residents mostly (residents of even a few hours can spot them, don't ask me how), which at least meant the desk wasn't too busy. I took the opportunity to book my wake-up call and my taxi to the airport then fought my way out front and asked the doorman to hail another cab to take me to the City University.

Every taxi I had seen since I arrived here was black or white or beige. The one that responded to the doorman's wave was violet. The doorman smiled. 'Lucky chance.'

There was a bear on the door he opened for me, dressed in a violet jersey.

'Sanfrecce,' he said. I nodded. It meant nothing. He leaned in and spoke to the driver, then tapped the roof to send us on our purply way.

When I looked back a couple of seconds later he was holding the door of a regular white taxi for a woman in a kimono and her husband in bow tie and tails. The doorman glanced up, over the couple's heads; touched his hat at me. I turned quickly away.

I tried not to dwell on the fact that I was being driven again, the day taken out of my hands. Or for that matter to dwell on the taxi driver's hands, in their tight-fitting white gloves. They all wore them. And none of them spoke to you, or encouraged your efforts to speak to them.

Traffic was beginning to build up. For almost a mile out of the city the speedometer barely got above twenty. We seemed to be paced by a relay of teenage schoolboys, in high-collared blazers and white trainers, on their black butcher's bikes. Some of them carried friends at the back, standing on what, I couldn't imagine, unless it was the wheel nuts. A few carried girlfriends. One girl held aloft a torn plastic flag, switching this way and that in the slipstream. It looked like the kind of thing you would get handed on Hondori – today a flag, tomorrow a heart-shaped balloon – though it hardly mattered what it was, its declaration was the same: they were a state unto themselves, him and her. The driver must have seen me in the mirror, looking. He said something at last, in English, I think. I didn't get the words, but I got the drift. To be young like that again.

'Yes,' I said to the envelope of his eyes. We shook our heads and carried on in a more companionable silence.

Out along the expressway, we drove, across a four-lane bridge, through the mountain tunnel finally, coming out on the far side at a tollgate.

Ahead of us was a van with three dogs disputing nose space at the rear grille. Labrador build without the breeding. They were the first dogs over a foot high I could remember seeing since arriving here. Something about the institutional look of the van, I didn't get the impression they were headed for a fun day in the mountains.

Fifty yards beyond the toll the expressway started to dip into the next valley. The dogs went down it barking, while we turned right and up a curving road, flanked by concrete embankments, towards the university. Even with the heavier traffic, it really had taken no time at all.

The campus was set on a deep shelf, behind which the mountain reared up more steeply, into a crown of dark green trees. The taxi indicated to pull in at the bottom of a broad flight of steps, but before it could stop, a man in a blue uniform stepped forward, blowing a whistle and waving us on. I was still looking over my shoulder at him when I heard the driver give a whistle of his own. Another uniformed man was directing us into a car park, at the end of which a crowd of a hundred or more was gathered, some shielding their eyes against the sun, watching our approach. Too grim for a welcome party, more like fifty arguments freeze-framed. Conference delegates, had to be. They watched as we drew up, ten yards short of them, watched as I paid the fare, forgetting in my fluster to ask for a receipt.

Maybe they had never seen a violet taxi either.

'Hi,' I said. I was scanning the faces for the only one I really knew.

I heard the taxi at my back drive away. The watching eyes didn't leave me, or at least didn't leave my right hand. The information pack. I held it up.

'U-bag,' I said. A hundred or more people flinched.

'It's OK. He's with me.'

I searched the faces again, but couldn't see who had spoken. I looked lower down. In a clearing between the legs, Ike sat on his maroon flight bag, smoking. (Smoking?)

The delegates turned away, resumed their discussions in jagged English.

'Have I come at a bad time?' I said, hunkering down myself beneath the babble.

Ike drew heavily on his cigarette. 'Don't ask.'

I didn't for maybe ten seconds. 'Some sort of drill?'

Ten seconds more. 'Bomb scare.'

'You're kidding.'

He looked at me from under a scowl. He wasn't.

'A parcel has been found. Strange shape, strange smell.'

I shielded my own eyes. Dražen, the Croatian, had suddenly materialised at my right shoulder, dressed now in shirt and jeans, but still wearing the bright green trainers.

'It's nonsense,' Ike said.

'Of course,' said Dražen and dropped to our level. 'It is the graffiti. It makes everyone nervous.'

There was no avoiding the question. 'Graffiti?' I said.

'All through the conference,' Dražen said. 'Sinister things.'

'Stupid things,' said Ike. '"You will be sorry for what you wrote." How many writers are there here? That's not a threat, that's a given.'

'Today was worse.'

'Today,' Ike came back, 'was even more stupid.'

'What?' I asked.

'"You know who you are",' Dražen recited.

'Like that's really sticking their neck out,' said Ike. 'It's a joke.'

Dražen shrugged, swaying on his heels. 'Nowadays it does not take much to frighten people.'

'Oh, come on, you know and I know that no one's seriously going to plant a bomb at a conference like this – in a place like this. We are probably in the safest city on earth.'

I couldn't quite fathom why, for someone so clearly un-impressed by the threat, he was acting so edgy. He crushed the cigarette under his shoe. There was an answering puff of air as the flight bag deflated a little more beneath him.

'I didn't have you pegged as a smoker,' I said.

'And we go so far back, the two of us,' he said, and if I had been a different person he might have got a dig in the bake for it. Was this the same guy who had phoned me earlier all chat and invitations?

There was movement around us, a making way. Dražen and I stood up. The shrubs bordering the car park merged with the tops of the trees growing up the side of the valley below, forming a dense green shield. A woman's voice was raised, headed in our direction.

'Klera Jaufenthaler? Olaf Salo? Has anyone seen Klera Jaufenthaler and Olaf Salo?'

Kimiko emerged behind a clipboard. Struggling, I would have said, to maintain her grip. She looked at me a moment, trying to place me.

'I'm sorry,' I said. Through a break in the hedge to her left I could see a bus turnaround with the siblings of the bus I should have got earlier today. 'This is probably the last thing you need, another person to keep track of.'

She barely acknowledged that I had spoken. I was not Klera Jaufenthaler. I was not Olaf Salo. That was all that concerned her at present. She pressed on through the crowd to our right. 'Klera Jaufenthaler and Olaf Salo? Has anyone seen Klera Jaufenthaler and Olaf Salo?'

'I saw Klera's husband.' Dražen directed the comment to Ike, still down among the legs. 'He is sick with worry. They were booked into different sessions this afternoon. He kissed her at the door of the auditorium, since when nothing.'

'I'm guessing we might have noticed two people being carted off against their will,' Ike said.

'Who said they were "carted off"? It is a big campus. They could have been persuaded into a room. Whoever is writing graffiti is here somewhere. It is not a Japanese problem, I don't think.'

'Whoever is writing the graffiti is having a laugh, end of story,' Ike said. I hadn't seen him take it out, but he had another cigarette in his mouth. He was just striking the match when the siren burst out from the background hum of traffic, headed our way. I turned, one of the audience now, to see a species of military fire engine slew to a halt at the steps where my taxi had first tried to pull in.

Ike threw down the match, as though that was the cause of the alarm. The cigarette was still hanging from his gaping mouth. He yanked it away, took a layer of bottom lip with it.

'Oh, for fuck's sake.'

He was on his feet, hands cupped over his mouth. Fire fighters in aluminium flash suits were jogging up the steps to the campus. Their officer, dressed a little less dramatically, though perhaps with a greater eye to self-preservation, in tunic and Kevlar hat, remained by the engine talking to Kimiko, who had run down in the meantime, clutching the clipboard to her chest.

'They've all gone fucking mad,' Ike said through his hand as another vehicle arrived in our car park. Another taxi. Black. I saw the bespectacled man get out slowly, try to take the whole scene in, as I had a few minutes before, though without the added strangeness of the fire engine.

'Olaf!' several dozen voices shouted; then several dozen more – one voice louder than the rest – shouted 'Klera!' as the offside rear door opened and a woman's head appeared, as though balanced on its pointed chin on the taxi's roof.

'Well, well,' said Ike grimly.

A man broke from our ranks and rounded the front of the taxi to Klera. His face was puce from the short run. He almost crumpled into her arms.

'Klera,' he said again, then added something in German, closing the door on most of those listening.

'I had a turn,' Klera said, for our benefit as much as his.

'Yes,' said Olaf – he had a tuft of hair over one ear that he seemed keen to flatten – 'a turn. I was on my way back from the toilets after lunch and I found her.'

'I didn't want to cause a fuss.' Klera looked past her husband, as I supposed the puce-faced man to be, at the very obvious, if disproportionate signs of fuss in the car park and beyond. 'Olaf very kindly got me back to the hotel.'

'I would have phoned,' Olaf said, 'but I thought we would be back before the end of the sessions. I didn't think that everyone would be waiting here, like this.'

'I bet you didn't,' Ike muttered at my ear, then instantly changed his tone. 'Olaf!'

Olaf had picked him out in the crowd and was striding towards him. 'I am so sorry … The traffic out of the city.' I said nothing. 'I didn't intend to miss your reading.'

Reading?

'You have not missed anything,' said Dražen to Olaf. 'It has been delayed. We have bomb scare.'

'You didn't tell me when you phoned you were giving a reading,' I said, wondering if that might account for the cigarettes, the wretched expression.

'The last of the conference,' Dražen said.

'I should have been finished by now,' said Ike. 'I should have been standing with a bloody great drink in my hand.'

Klera's husband had been clinging to her all this time, still talking to her alone. Now he took a step back.

'Oh, Klera!' his voice rang with disappointment. He dragged his fingers down his cheeks to his chin.

Klera's own face reddened. 'But, Walter, I thought you knew.'

'How could I know?' He was turning circles. 'Somebody,' he said. 'Kimiko.'

Kimiko had just arrived back in the car park, a little out of breath. 'What is it?'

'The parcel,' said Klera.

'The strange shape and smell,' said Walter.

'It is a cake. An Austrian cake with marzipan icing. I found it in one of the patisseries.'

'Oh, Klera,' Walter said, but Kimiko was already off again, running towards the fire engine.

She talked to the officer, who took out his radio and turned his back. A couple of minutes later his men came down the broad steps, flash suit hoods already draped over their arms, and handed Kimiko a loaf-shaped package wrapped up in a carrier bag. When the fire engine had departed, with a final *whup* of its siren to warn oncoming cars, and – who knows? – careless cake owners, Kimiko walked back as dignifiedly as someone could who had just had to expend a hundred bows of deepest apology and gave the package to Klera.

'See?' Klera said, unfolding the bag so that she held it by the handles. It had a picture of a patisserie on the front, a little piece of Old Vienna. 'It was to be a joke present: a souvenir of Japan.'

If only it had been in a U-bag, the confusion need never have arisen.

Up on the campus an electric bell was sounding the all clear. A bus engine started up. Around me the delegates were growing restless. Stand-up discussions were all very well, but how much better with chairs – with a Chair!

Kimiko had withdrawn with Ike to one side of the car park. He listened in silence while she talked. A slight nod of his head. A long pause. (Even at a distance his lip looked swollen, pouty.) Another slight nod then a third, more emphatic. Kimiko seized both his wrists, a gesture of immense gratitude. She turned, clapped her hands.

'Friends! Friends! Your attention one moment! Thank you. You know, I am sure, that the mayor of Hiroshima has graciously agreed to join us at this evening's reception. You know, too, that we were to have enjoyed before that a very special reading.'

There was some small applause at the mere mention of it, one call of 'Author! Author!'.

Kimiko raised her hand. Her smile said no one would be disappointed.

'The mayor's schedule, you understand, is very tight. So we will proceed with the reception as planned, but' – she raised the hand higher, spread the fingers – 'I am delighted to be able to tell you that, by the most kind agreement of our distinguished colleague, we will have our reading immediately afterwards in the auditorium.'

The applause this time was widespread and determined, even a touch defiant. The conference had been put to the test – by a cake, but who could have known? – and had emerged stronger, more united. Dražen slapped Ike on the back and was rewarded with a squinty smile that quickly retracted to fat-lipped pout.

Kimiko was attempting to say something more – I caught the words 'appetite' and 'main course' – but already, on all sides, the movement had begun out of the car park. I heard Olaf's voice, too, still talking about the traffic, about Klera's funny turn, but mostly all I got was gabble.

Students in Writing Out of Conflict T-shirts patrolled the edges of the migration, to make sure none of the delegates strayed off course or got mixed up with the groups I saw now returning to the campus from assembly positions in car parks higher up. It seemed it didn't matter whether you were dealing with Korean pensioners or eminent writers and academics, a point was reached, and sooner than we cared to think, where the group became a herd. Instinct alone would probably have dictated that I follow, but business sense surfaced to clinch it: the mayor was going to be there. I had been chasing around Hiroshima for a week trying to engineer a meeting and now he was to be served up on a buffet plate.

'So' – Dražen was beside me – 'you have decided to join us?'

In the circumstances it was as near to a confirmed invitation as I was likely to get.

'For a while at least,' I said.

'Home in the morning,' he said, as though he could have written the script himself.

'Home in the morning,' I echoed.

Ike trailed behind us, smoking a long, white cigarette – an altogether different brand from the ones he had been smoking earlier – holding the strap of his maroon flight bag for dear life.

The university buildings were a variation on the sixties campus-theme of red brick, glass, and raised concrete walkways. There was the odd distinctive touch, but what really set Hiroshima City apart was the spaces between the buildings, the sudden, staggering views, of receding mountain ranges in one direction, the undulating outline of the Big Arch football stadium across the valley in another. (Of course: *Sanfrecce* – the bear in the violet jersey. I'd been driven here in an ad for Hiroshima's J-Leaguers.)

I followed the herd along the front of the auditorium housing the conference. As Ike had suggested, I would have had no trouble finding it. Every other window carried a poster of the pen bursting out of its shell. A conference bulletin board just inside the main doors had a picture of Ike in a younger man's body and a starting time beneath it that was likewise already history.

Outside, a few yards further on, the concrete wall bore the marks of recent power-hosing. Graffiti removal. As so often happens, though, the very precision of the treatment only invited you to fill in the blanks, drawing more attention to the words.

'You know who you are.'

I was with Ike on this. Whoever was doing it wasn't making any great claims.

Our trek terminated, after – gasp! – one more glimpse of distant hills, on the ground floor of the grandly named, but greyly built, Student Hall. The volunteers had formed two loose lines either side of a double doorway, to the left of a central flight of steps: less guard of honour, more human funnel.

Tadao was in the middle right. He seemed surprised to see me, but did his bow as I passed all the same. I would have bowed back if I hadn't known his eyes had probably already turned Ikewards.

Immediately through the doors was a bookstall, manned by a mountainous rockabilly, with a tiger baring its teeth just below one shoulder of his sleeveless checked shirt. The stock was mostly journals, mostly in two-tone matt jackets (*Trade and Labelling* would not have looked out of place) and, like the conversation around me, mostly in English. I cast my eye over the small stock of actual books searching for something, anything, of Ike's. I didn't imagine his having to search as hard as I was having to would do much to improve his humour. Then the stallman shifted his bulk to serve someone else and I saw in the space he had abandoned two unopened cartons on the floor, 'Hurts' written on their sides in black marker.

I turned in time to see Ike enter and walk past the stall as though it wasn't there; except the stall, like the erased graffiti earlier, seemed all the more potent for being blanked.

The drinks table was next to the bookstall and half the size again. Red and white wine, both kinds of water and very vivid orange juice. Dražen, ahead of me, lifted a sparkling water. My hand hovered over a white wine, then went for water too: the herd thing again, but there was the reading to think of as well. Who knew how hard it might be to keep my eyes open, even without two or three glasses of Sauvignon Blanc dragging on the lids?

When the last of the delegates was inside, the students appeared again to channel us, glasses in hand, through a deserted cafeteria and on into a more open area, across which men and women in black waistcoats were carrying stainless steel platters to a wall-length buffet, causing a polite bottleneck to form near the entrance and causing me, separated all of a sudden from Dražen as well as Ike, to mingle whether I wanted to or not.

I found myself talking to an Armenian man, who, when I asked if he was a writer said, no, a thinker, and didn't blush, and who got it into his head that I wrapped food as an artistic statement.

'Like Christo, yes?' he said. 'Only smaller.'

From then on if anyone asked what I did I said I was an observer, which seemed to satisfy them. I decided too after that conversation with the Armenian to abandon the water. The white wine was bone dry. The first sip bypassed my tongue completely and pinged at the junction of my throat and ears. I grimaced. The second sip was easier, the third easier still.

A Canadian (he wore one of those maple leaf lapel pins they are issued with at birth) shook my hand.

'I believe you're a compatriot of the Great Man,' he said.

He had a leathery face, rings in his long, loose lobes that were closer to eyelets: windows on to where he had been the second before.

'Assuming you mean who I think you mean, yes,' I said. 'I am.'

He laughed. His teeth were newer than his lapel pin. 'Now I know you are for sure: the Irish sense of humour.'

The first time I had been accused of it and I hadn't even been trying.

'I missed him last year in San Francisco,' the Canadian went on. 'So you can imagine when I saw his name on the advance publicity for this I made damned sure and signed up straight away.'

I will admit it wasn't the easiest thing I had ever had to imagine. I had a quick look around the room, but couldn't see His Greatness.

The Canadian said something about suffering.

'I beg your pardon?'

'I said, he's so good on suffering. But then, I guess that's another thing, being Irish …'

He left the thought dangling before me. I tried to fashion a great big stick of a reply with which to whack it out the window and clear over the mountain behind us.

'I don't know about that,' was the best I could come up with.

He smiled at my modesty. We sipped our wine. The stainless steel platters were still being brought out, but though the delegates appeared to be hanging back they had somehow managed to close in on the tables. It was like the game we used to play when we were kids, *One-two-three, red light!* The object was not to be seen to be moving.

I scanned the faces. Suddenly, from nowhere, I had my stick.

'Is this everyone?' I asked.

'Everyone?'

'Who's attending the conference?'

The Canadian looked about him. 'Pretty much, yes.'

'Oh.'

'What?'

'Well, you don't think it's a bit …' I saw in my mind's eye the men in pink pyjamas mute on the hotel news channel, the row of skulls they helped create, 'I don't know, *pale?*'

The Canadian regarded me a moment as though repartitioning a mental map. 'I get what you're saying, and I agree, it's a shame.' He set his glass down on a ledge and offered me his hand again. 'Nice talking to you.'

'And you,' I said to his back. I had finished my wine. There was a scrum around the drinks table. I lifted the Canadian's glass from the ledge. The empty side of half. This, and that would be me till after the reading.

I was raising the glass to my lips when I felt a hand on my shoulder. Ike, I thought, and turned to find the Canadian.

'Oh, listen,' I said, making to hand back the wine.

He shook his head. 'A couple of years ago,' he said, 'Melbourne. There was a delegate, a doctorate student, from Liberia. His family had pooled their money to pay his flight and conference fees. He nearly didn't make it to the airport: ran into a roadblock. A gang of kids with guns. They emptied out his luggage at the side of the road looking for cash. He arrived with only what he stood up in. When it came time to give his paper he could hardly speak for sobbing.'

'What did the audience do?'

'We did our best.' The Canadian dropped his voice. 'There were only five of us. And do you know the worst about it? It wasn't even a very good paper. He submitted it for the journal, but ...' He spread his hands. 'The editor is pretty rigorous. You know: you make allowance for one, where do you stop?'

'And did he, I mean, getting home again ... Was he OK?'

'Oh, sure. I mean we email.' He drew the 'e' out to its maximum length. You could hear the beginning of eternity in it; you could hear no end of regret. Maybe I had got the Canadian all wrong.

'And now,' he said, 'if you don't mind, I'm going to get something to eat.'

While my back had been turned – *one-two-three, red light!* – the delegates had finally reached the tables. They didn't care now about being seen to move, didn't appear to care much either about what anyone thought of their selection. The conference buffet differs from the breakfast buffet in this crucial respect: everyone proceeds on the understanding that the only limit is plate size.

The centrepiece this evening was a whole salmon on ice. The skin had been cut crossways and peeled back. The eye looked barely dimmed, so that thoughts of autopsy were succeeded by thoughts of operations gone wrong, of a patient just this minute expired upon the table.

'It doesn't come much fresher than that,' a woman behind me said admiringly.

When I was a student the hottest curry was the grail, now, even in Belfast, it was the Freshest Sashimi You Will Ever Eat. I had been offered it three or four times a day since arriving here. On my second day in Tokyo I had joined a bus party, forty strong at five a.m., to the city's wholesale fish market. Breakfast was included in the price. Sashimi naturally. En route, along the deserted streets of Ginza, we were fed the statistics: the acreage, the tonnage, the number of species, though no amount of forewarning could prepare anyone for the frozen tuna auction. (The fresh tuna, we had been told, would have been sold long before we, or any other bus party, arrived.) Jobbers with ice picks tucked in their belts moved among the hundreds of carcasses – great frosted torpedoes, shorn of fins and tails – dropping to their knees now and then to chip a piece out for inspection; auctioneers' assistants painted the buyer's name in red on the fishes' sides, and motorised trolleys whisked them to the surrounding stalls to be sawn into steaks and sold on. And this scene was repeated six days out of every seven, fifty-two weeks a year. I knew little of the tuna other than what I had read on tins, but it was hard not to think of whole underwater neighbourhoods lying empty, seaweed tumbling down avenues of barren rock.

Our bus party was leaving the auction hall, heading for breakfast, when I almost tripped over a pallet bearing two of the fresh tuna auctioned earlier. After so much frozen fish, their full-blooded meatiness alone would have been shocking, but what was worse, the severed tails were sticking out of their mouths. Vendetta, I thought, and before I could check it a memory surfaced, from way back, of a guy from round our way, shot and dumped in a supermarket loading bay, his balls and all, the rumour went, stuffed into his mouth. Another rumour went further: a note tucked under his gory chin, 'Bet you always wanted to do that'.

I passed that morning on the freshest sashimi I would ever eat. I passed on the salmon at the reception. I concentrated instead on the tempura, trying to memorise the four different kinds of salt with which it was served: Izu, Okinawa, Yamaguchi, Hiroshima.

I could see Norma, her brow wrinkling as I told her over lunch. '*Salt?*'

2

We had been filling our plates for half an hour when the police arrived: plainclothes, which is to say as inconspicuous as ink in water as they moved among us in their bulked-out suits and narrow ties. News of the bomb scare was clearly not being taken lightly downtown. Only when the plainclothesmen were satisfied they had one hundred and some conference delegates well covered and all the sushi knives in view did they give the signal for the mayor to enter. The mayor entered as though he didn't know he had been preceded by police, as though he hadn't broken stride all day, except to shake hands, as he shook hands now, left and right, on his way to the podium that had materialised at the far end of the room, where he adjusted his tie and announced, in the breath after 'Good evening and welcome', that he would be at the UN headquarters in New York later in the month. (He wasn't entirely unacquainted with that part of the world if his accent was any guide.) He wanted the delegates gathered here to know that they made a much more daunting audience than any he would face there.

The delegates' murmuring could not have sounded less daunting, more purr-like.

The mayor made a few more comments of a kind not generally heard at Plasticised PVC Packaging conferences, about the keeping of conscience and legislating without acknowledgement. He talked about the Peace Bell, in the grounds of the A-Bomb Museum. Every day, he said, hundreds of people stepped up to ring the bell: people from all corners of the world engraved without borders on the bell's casting. For each one it was an act of immense significance; for some it was what they had travelled the thousands of miles to Japan to do, putting aside money for months, perhaps even years. And yet, depending on the wind, the traffic, their own preoccupations, pedestrians walking across Aioi Bridge a mere fifty metres away might not hear a particular strike at all, or if they heard it might not be able to tell it from the one that went before, from the one that would inevitably follow, as the next person came forward to swing the hammer. But if ever the bell were to stop ringing altogether, the people of Hiroshima would know, the world would know.

They liked that too, the delegates, the unspoken comparison. They applauded it soundly with their bell-ringers' hands. The mayor bowed to them, wished them well in their endeavours, wherever Writing Out of Conflict would take them next, bowed again, then at the same pace as he had entered started back through the room to the exit.

I didn't know I was going to do it till I did it.

'Mr Mayor,' I said, as he drew level. I held out my U-bag. 'A gift from Belfast.'

An aide made a move for it, but I extended my arm the extra few inches and delivered the bag into the mayor's hands, chest level. He was still walking, so I walked too. There were two guys breathing down my neck.

'From Belfast Ireland?' the mayor said.

'From Belfast Ireland. The best thing from the city, we like to say, since the wheel.'

He was turning the pack over in his hands, a sachet of hot chocolate from one of our top restaurateurs, a Katie Melua CD.

'The wheel?' he said.

(Katie Melua? he might have said. Lived in Belfast between the ages of nine and fourteen.)

'It's all in the pack, along with my card. I'm here again in November …'

He was out the door, the aides and plainclothesmen behind him, but it didn't matter, it could go in the report: *informal meeting with mayor*. I had done everything now I had come to Hiroshima to do.

A few moments later the door opened again and a troop of middle-aged men in dinner jackets and bow ties passed before me. Like plainclothes police, male voice choirs are impossible to confuse with any other group of similarly dressed men. Something in the smile, maybe, a recognition that this was not what you had been banking on, but here they were and there you were and what else could you all do?

They formed two rows of ten (the conductor splayed his forefinger and thumb, encouraging them to smile with more conviction), before launching into 'Imagine', their voices dwindling to a whisper on 'dreamer', then rising in volume again; up and then down, up and then down and then up to a final, ringing 'as one'. They sang 'Bridge Over Troubled Water', followed by a couple of things I didn't recognise or even understand, though in the course of the second I saw Dražen, across the room, rub below one widened eye then the other. Then they cleared their throats and I thought, here comes 'Danny Boy', a second before they hit the opening *O*.

I looked around for Ike – was it me or had he seen it coming too? Heard it, I mean: a telltale range-finding note amid the throat clearing. But he was nowhere to be found. In fact, I couldn't remember seeing him at all since he passed me at the bookstall. My eye roved back and forth a few minutes longer, lingering on the most likely places – drinks table, buffet, toilet doors. When there was still no sign of him I worked my way through the throng, broadening my search. I spotted him eventually, alone, on the far side of the cafeteria. The lights had not been switched on here and the sky outside was shading from dark blue into black. He was sitting right beside the window, in a patch of cornered daylight, head angled towards the glass. He had the books out of the flight bag and spread in an arc before him, their yellow and orange and pink Post Its stuck all about the tabletop. I stopped, twenty feet short. He had the black notebook out too and hunched over it to scribble something with his pencil, looking for all the world like someone trying to cram his revision into the final hour before the exam; looking, actually, like the nerves were really getting to him. There were three empty glasses on the windowsill, a fourth, well begun, by his left elbow.

I went and found Dražen, brought him in for a second long-range opinion.

'Is he OK do you think?'

Dražen moved his head left and right, covering all the angles.

'That is how he is before readings. Maybe not so grey, but then maybe that's the light.' He guided me by the arm, as though away from something that was beyond mere human understanding. 'Come. Let him do what he has to do.'

I slipped his grip. A less polite person would have told him to catch himself on, it was reading from a book, for dear sake. Ike wanted to try doing a PowerPoint presentation to a roomful of executives on someone else's computer.

The choir was still singing. 'Blowin' In the Wind'. Some of the delegates were joining in, swaying with the words. A platoon of waiters moved among them with fresh trays of drinks. The first wave was wiped out in seconds. It took a third wave to reach the delegates still at the buffet. I had a last glance over my shoulder. Ike was more than ever sunk in gloom.

The choir sang 'If I Had a Hammer'. The delegates clapped their free hands on their thighs. 'Justice,' they hollered, 'Freedom,' and then, 'Love between all of my brothers and my sisters, all over this land.'

Kimiko, when the song had finished and the thigh-clapping and foot-stamping and whistling had begun to abate, came forward to stand by the conductor and called the room to order.

'Thank you. Thank you,' she said to, or maybe on behalf of, the choir. 'Now could I ask you all to be so kind as to make your way to the auditorium?'

I sensed a shift in the mood since she had addressed us in the car park, a disappointment that this part of the evening was ending so soon.

'And –' Kimiko made an exclamation mark of her forefinger – 'could you, *please*, be sure to bring all your belongings.'

Walter Jaufenthaler held the Old Vienna cake bag aloft and was rewarded with a cheer. He squeezed his wife to his side. Even Klera was forgiven in the afterglow of the hammer song.

I left just behind Dražen. As we passed through the cafeteria, Ike appeared from the shadows and fell in at his side.

'I've been thinking,' he said, 'the mood they're all in, I'm just going to read one bit.'

Dražen nodded with his consultant's gravitas. 'I think that is an excellent idea.'

'Yeah?' The swelling on Ike's lip had gone right down, but his speech still sounded a little thick. 'That's what I'll do then. I was thinking the passage from *Hurts*, you know, with Nell.'

'Excellent.'

Ike dived into the flight bag again, yanking the mouth this way and that until he was satisfied that, the decision made, he had remembered to pick the book up from the cafeteria table.

Lights were coming on down in the valley and forming little

constellations on the mountainsides beyond. The Big Arch stadium was lit like a vast space ship. *Go, Sanfrecce. Go.*

At the entrance to the auditorium Ike was singled out and taken through his own private door. There was a clay sculpture in the foyer, a head and trunk lashed to a rough post. The expression on the face was only marginally unhappier than Ike's as he was led away from us.

I told Dražen how impressed I was that he knew which passage Ike had been referring to by just two words, 'with Nell'.

'You have never heard him read before?' he asked, as though it somehow followed on.

'No,' I said, 'but then I've never been in Belfast Cathedral.'

He turned to face me. Clearly I wasn't the only one having trouble keeping track of the conversation.

'You know, when you go away, what's top of your list of things to see?'

Dražen nodded slowly, slowly. I couldn't tell whether he was testing my theory or simply searching for the words to reply. I was none the wiser by the time we were let into the auditorium, though he was still giving me the odd nod. If even a fraction of the delegates were like him it was no wonder they had to have so many Writing Out of Conflict conferences. In fact the wonder was that they could ever decide where to meet next.

The auditorium was so vast that the delegates, conference staff and volunteers filled barely a third. They left the front four rows entirely empty, but even then there was plenty of scope further back for lounging, *sprawling.* Ike's exclusive door had simply got him into the hall faster, so that he had to hang around now at the side of the platform while people arranged their coats and bags, found friends who had kept them a seat, made last-minute dashes forwards, or, more often, back. Quite a number had ignored the notice on the door saying No Food or Drink Beyond This Point. Or had ignored the second half of it anyway. The lights were bright, but without warmth. It would have put you in mind of early summer evenings at home, people sitting outside bars, blue with cold, grimly insistent on extracting the most out of the day, even a little fun if it came their way.

Kimiko walked to the microphone. (The more I saw, the more I realised it was Kimiko's show.) She had a few announcements about tomorrow's events, which she would try to get through as quickly as possible. There had been a mistake in their programmes. The conference summary and closing address would, of course, take place in this auditorium at ten o'clock – that's ten hundred hours – and not o-one-hundred as printed. This would be followed, for those who did not have to leave straightaway, by a picnic lunch at the magnificent temple complex at Miya-jima (bento boxes could be collected from the cafeteria). I glanced at Dražen. Cathedrals, temple complexes, same difference, I tried to make my eyes say. His nod was practically time-lapse.

A little man with large glasses and a loud check jacket came forward and asked could he make a short announcement about papers for publication. Five minutes later, having given the email addresses twice, the absolute latest deadline for submissions three times, and fielded half a dozen questions, he was just threatening a final recap when Kimiko interrupted. Perhaps they could return to the subject tomorrow morning?

'Yes, of course, yes, sorry.'

It occurred to me this was the journal editor the Canadian had spoken of. He picked up his sheet of email addresses and dates and backed away, casting covetous looks at the lectern as he went, at Kimiko positioned between it and him.

'Well, it has been Some Day,' she said and smiled, mistress of idiomatic understatement. 'In fact, I don't want to do the job of tomorrow's summariser, but, speaking only for myself, it has been Some Conference. I feel honoured to have been involved. The reading we are about to hear, however, is one I have been looking forward to since we started putting the programme together last spring. I suppose you could say it is' – the smile again – 'Some Way To End. For me, it is really the only way.'

I hadn't noticed Ike take his seat, but I noticed him now get to his feet again, prematurely. He didn't look the steadiest. He crouched as though to sit back down and then seemed to decide he was better off walking. Seeing him lurch towards the platform, Kimiko speeded up her introduction. She got to his name as he got to the top of the steps. The applause didn't exactly sweep her aside. The delegates were all sunk too far down in their seats.

Ike's hand shook as he took a bottle of mineral water from beneath the lectern and unscrewed the top. The sound of his swallowing carried through the auditorium. It went on. And on. When the glass was empty he poured himself a refill and set it back noisily on the lower shelf.

'Hello there,' he said and even in those three syllables you could hear something wasn't right. He had only one book now. He bent the back two or three times, though its resistance had been broken a long time ago. A page with a pink Post It attached wafted towards the floor. He caught it at the second attempt, put it back in the book, then took it out and turned it the right way up. Someone behind me stifled a laugh. Ike peered against the glare into the auditorium. The control room finally dimmed the lights a little. He blinked, adjusting, spotlighted still from above. His hair was going at the crown, faster perhaps than he was aware.

'Um,' he said. 'I, um, OK. I'm going to read a passage from a novel called *Hurts*.' He gave the spine another tweak. 'It's, well, it's from near the middle, so a couple of things maybe you should know. Let's see.'

He stared down at the page as though at a confession he could not remember making. I thought, this is just plain cruel. The man is no fit state.

'A ferret,' he said, 'is an army vehicle. So is a pig. A budgie is a wee bird you keep in a cage and all blue-eyed white cats are deaf. Well, all blue-eyed white Irish cats. *Northern* Irish. Well, this blue-eyed, white Northern Irish cat is anyway.'

He sipped his water. The shake wasn't as bad as it had been.

'What else? The characters' lives, you won't be surprised to hear, are a lot more complicated than they were at the start of the novel, and, the most important thing of all you have to know, this passage will take me' – watch off, band around his fingers – 'fourteen minutes and forty seconds to read.

'So,' another sip, '*Hurts.*'

He gripped the sides of the lectern as he began to read, his index fingers tapping a beat that was inaudible to me in his words. The mood in the theatre had softened. The cat quip had helped, the time limit even more. People still lounged and drank, four rows and further away from him, but you sensed they were prepared to make the mental leap, to be on his side, at least for fourteen minutes and forty seconds.

There were a couple more mild laughs in the opening paragraphs. It was all much more domestic than some of his introduction would have led you to believe. A woman – Nell – in her kitchen, redding out the cupboards. I wondered at the use of that term, 'redding out', uncommon now even at home, wondered that there was no explanation for anyone who had never heard it. There was not a sniff of a ferret, or a pig either, though the budgie was there, hanging sideways from the bars of its cage, in imitation, Ike hinted, of its plastic 'mate', which had listed to the left from the day and hour it was hooked to its perch.

I was trying to get a handle on when this was supposed to be set. Some of the references – products, decor – suggested early eighties, but then at the back of one cupboard, behind the Mellow Bird's was a bottle of Camp Coffee, which didn't sound quite in keeping. He went into great detail (too much detail?) about the label: a kilted army officer seated on a drum, a saucer in one hand, a cup in the other, a connoisseur's concentrated expression on his face; beside him, and a little withdrawn, his Indian manservant, awaiting approval; at their backs a ludicrously not-to-scale tent ('unless it's supposed to be a latrine'), a pennant at the top with the motto, 'Ready, Aye Ready'.

The bottle was glued shut by the residue of coffee around the lid. It hadn't been opened in years.

He looked up as he said this and I felt a curious need to be seen to be smiling. I got it now, all the detail. The motto and the gummy lid weren't half as good without it. And though the bottle itself had seemed out of place to begin with, he was right, it was exactly the kind of thing you did find, years later, pushed to the back of a cupboard.

His eyes, however, simply skimmed the surface of the audience, and besides, I got the impression I wasn't the only one smiling. (Did it matter that you had never seen a Camp Coffee bottle? That you didn't know it for the sugary gloop that it was?) He looked down again, frowning slightly, as though he had nearly let himself forget where he was. The fingers tapped. Someone placed their hands over Nell's eyes. Her heart seemed to stop … start again, twice as fast.

'Ready?' a man's voice said close to the back of her head.

She didn't reply straight off.

'Aye,' she said then, a shy Belfast yes, 'ready.'

With her eyes still covered she stretched forward to tilt the kitchen blinds and her groin pressed against the sink. She made a small noise. That was all he said, a small noise, but I heard it just the same – almost, for a moment, had a face to go with it. The man asked her should they move and she said she was happy to stay right where she was, on tiptoe, leaning into the rim of the sink, him tucked in behind her – he'd be surprised how long she'd be happy to stay like that. But of course even in saying the words she was guaranteeing that they would not stay as they were, that there would be movement, slight to begin with, localised; guaranteeing that she would want to turn around eventually, take his face in her hands, kiss it hungrily, like this, like this, like this; staggering him.

They bounced off the cooker, the countertop, the cupboard

doors, feeling with their hands and their backsides for a place to come to rest: not the little card table in the corner, that's for sure, and not the fridge, with all its bumps and clunks and disturbed electricity and finally a crash – later, later – just not the fridge.

I was trying not to and then I was laughing, short blasts – mercifully silent, mercifully dry – down my nose. Don't ask me what was so funny. I mean, if you had stopped to think about it, there were no actual jokes; but that was the problem, if laughing was a problem, there was no room between the lines to think. The couple staggered from card table to fridge to countertop again, colliding with the budgie cage on the way (the budgie was going totally loopy, even its plastic mate was bouncing) and it was seriously funny.

Then they were on the floor. There was dirt down there: Special K, fruit pips, tomato spiders (*yes*, I thought, that's just what they are), a pool of water from an unidentified source, rimed with dust and hair. And what they were doing down there, or how Ike was telling us what they were doing, or how he was telling us they were telling each other, that was dirty too: words increasingly of one syllable, as though breath was too precious to waste on speech.

Ike looked up again. It was shocking what was coming out of his mouth, but somehow he gave the impression that he was not responsible for it.

The white cat had wandered in and like a sitcom guest star got a laugh just for appearing. It passed Nell and her man as though they weren't there, eyes only for the dish beneath the card table. The man was hissing in Nell's ear, 'Wait … cat … door … quick … be- … fore … uh …' but she was telling him to leave it, please, leave it. Ike was holding the book a little off the lectern, passing on the words, the cat's head slowly turning, a drip on its chin, taking in the scene with its blue eyes. Standing then, arching as it brought the rest of its body round, hunching down again.

'What's it doing?'

The man was trying to see over his shoulder. Nell was turning his face with her hands, pulling him down.

'There,' she was saying. 'There.'

Ike was barely glancing at the book at all now. He had focused on a point three rows in front of me: a woman and a man, sitting side by side, empty seats to their left and right. The Jaufenthalers, I thought, though I couldn't see their faces to confirm it. The woman's shoulders were quivering. The man's ears were red, the back of his neck was red, but there was a tremor in his shoulders too. From behind, it was clear that they were unaware of one another's reaction. In that moment they were closer to Ike, fifty feet away, than they were to each other. Suddenly it dawned on me how he was able to stand up there and say all that stuff: he had made it their problem – our problem – not his.

The cat's head was weaving, trying to get a clear view. Its tail swished on the floor, knocking against the chair, which knocked against the card table, which rattled the cup and saucer left there from breakfast.

'Oh, fuck, oh, fuck, oh, fuck,' Ike said Nell said and then the cat's paw shot out.

'Fuck!' yelled the man. 'Kick it!'

'*Leave it.*'

'Ow!'

'*Oh!*'

'Ow!'

'*Oh!*'

Nell and the man couldn't stop, the cat couldn't stop, the couple in front of me, shoulders shaking, ears sizzling, couldn't stop. Ike stopped. He looked down at the book. The frown returned. Something was not right. I was aware that I was frowning too. The card table, the single chair, the single cup and saucer … Ike took a sip of water, scarcely missing a beat, though some of us in that split second caught up with what he was about to say – almost – as the words were leaving his mouth. There weren't two people in the kitchen. The blinds were closed, but Nell hadn't moved from the sink. She opened her eyes. The cat was hunched beneath the card table, tail flicking. The cup rattled on the saucer.

So what was all that about earlier? Fantasy? Memory? Some mingling of the two? It was a cheat, that was for sure.

Nell stood pressed against the rim of the sink with the Camp Coffee bottle in her hand, tears running down her cheeks. She twisted the lid until it came unstuck, catching her breath against the too-sweet chicory reek, and tipped the bottle over the plughole. When there was nothing left to pour out, she chucked the bottle in the pedal bin to the right of the card table. The budgie trilled over the hi-hat beat of its own feet on the cage bars.

The ferrets and the pigs were over the page. Ike smoothed it flat with a gesture that implied he would not be turning another one. He had slipped the watch back over his wrist. The clock on the wall showed thirteen minutes had already elapsed. The ferrets and pigs formed a cordon through which Nell walked – *remembered* walking: he was explicit now – a link in a chain completed by her sister and a policewoman, to the end of the street where the body lay, covered by a sheet.

'Be strong,' she said in her head, over and over. 'Be strong.'

She noticed every speck of dirt on the ground. She was angry that they hadn't had the decency to clean the street for him, neither the police nor the men who had decided that, due to a congruence of historical and political circumstance to which only they were privy, this was where his life would end, and who had hung around in the darkness – because they were reasonable like that, they didn't mind waiting – to deliver the news. Which, even they must have known, was a blow that nothing could soften – not their reasonableness, not their carefully calculated justification, least of all what they prided themselves was the brisk professionalism of their delivery. Bam: that's that then.

The chewing gum was a particular vexation. The chewing gum looked like the residue of some freak meteorological event. Nell swore she would never let another stick pass her lips.

She didn't recognise the blood as blood in the spillage of street lighting. She didn't associate then the matter mixed through it with the brain that could decide while he sat in traffic en route to work that today had just been declared a holiday and that would carry the thought across the city to her door. Ready?

Aye, ready.

'Be strong,' she repeated and tightened her grip on her sister's arm. 'Be strong.'

The instant the sheet was pulled back her sister collapsed between Nell and the policewoman. It was left to Nell to speak the words, though really the issue had not been in doubt, from the moment her sister rang early this winter evening, hysterical.

'That's him.' *Be strong. Be strong.* 'That's my brother-in-law.'

3

For a few moments after he closed the book, nothing happened, then the applause began, rapidly, as though to make up for the pause. It seemed to overtake itself, if such a thing was possible, becoming a percussionless roar. I couldn't even hear my own contribution, though I clapped till my hands were sore, and then some, till they were two bits of bony meat I had picked up on the sticks of my arms and was flapping ineffectually in front of me.

Dražen leaned across to me. 'Well?' he asked.

'I don't know what to say.'

And I didn't, truly. At some point I had lost sight of my surroundings, had lost sight too of the fact that this was not the sort of thing I liked. I was on that street, offended by the litter, prepared for the worst; prepared for anything except that final sentence.

The applause was at last dying down. Ike was crouching to shake hands with delegates who had clambered over the rows of empty seats to the front. Books were being passed up to him.

Kimiko was on the platform again. She looked like she had just rushed back from the same street I had been on.

'Colleagues, friends, if you would like to have your books signed could you please make your way to the stall in the foyer?'

She waited while Ike signed one more where he stood then ushered him off the platform and out his private door. I knew then how I would carry back his autograph for Tom and Jill. (Would they wonder at me when they got to that passage, down there on the kitchen floor?)

By the time I was able to get out of my row and down the stairs, however, the queue from the foyer was already stretching back into the auditorium. It moved forward slowly. At the far end of it, Ike sat, a pile of books to his right, pen at the ready, though as often as not when I glanced round the woman's head in front of me he seemed to be deep in conversation with whoever had offered up their book to be signed.

I would watch the person afterwards walk a few feet from the table before flicking back the cover to see what he had written: the bare minimum, the expressions seemed to say, after all that chat.

The rockabilly bookseller replenished the pile from the boxes I had seen earlier inside the cafeteria doors. The queue moved forward, the pile got smaller, then bigger, then smaller again. One box was collapsed, the other opened; books were added to the pile and just as quickly lifted off to be signed. The queue moved forward, the second box was collapsed. A couple of people behind me gave up. I counted the heads between me and the signing table, had a stab at the number of books remaining, and decided to hang in there. I got the maths absolutely right. There were two books left on the table when the woman ahead of me stepped forward. She lifted them both.

'I've been trying to get hold of your earlier books for the longest time,' she said. Her accent was naturalised American. 'I tried in my campus bookstore then I tried all the chains. Even the online out-of-print specialists had problems finding them. Well, at a price that wasn't, like, you know …'

She snorted. Ike's smile drew in slightly; his attention wavered. He looked past the woman and saw me. He looked at the books she had given him, did his own calculation. I held up my hand to say it didn't matter. He held up his hand to keep the woman from launching in again.

'Excuse me,' he said to her, then to me: 'Listen, if you hold on another minute I'm sure I can sort something out.'

The woman cast a cold eye over me – who was I eating into her time? – then turned back to him. 'One of the stores I went into to ask about you told me there was no such person. I'm going to go straight round there when I get home and wave these in their faces.'

She demonstrated, close to Ike's face, then raised the book in the left hand a little higher than the one on the right.

'This is for my partner, Sal, spelt exactly like it sounds.' She raised the right hand. 'This is for me. I don't like anybody else touching mine, even Sal. It's Orsola. Spelt …'

'With an A at one end only,' said Ike, clicking his pen, keen to get this over with.

'Excuse me?'

When she had gone, pausing twice as long as most, to glance inside both books, looking twice as unimpressed, he folded his arms on the table and laid his head on top of them.

'There is no distance too great for some people to travel to remind you how unsuccessful you are.'

'You could hardly call that in there unsuccessful,' I said.

He raised his head. 'You thought the passage worked OK?'

Either he really was uncertain or he just wanted to hear it free from even the whiff of a negative.

'It was great,' I said. 'I don't mind telling you I was surprised.'

'Thank you, and how far have you come today?'

I didn't see anything to apologise for. 'I thought you were going to keel over before you even began. You looked a state.'

'Yeah, well.' He was on his feet now, stretching, the day's work done. The bloody great drink had been delivered, gin or vodka, double or even treble. 'You know what they say about books and covers.'

I knew what they said too about kidding a kidder, but I let it pass. He wandered off to find the bookstall guy. He was gone one minute, two minutes, three. I rested one bum-cheek on the edge of the table, which wobbled. I sat, sideways, on the chair, but it was hard not to slip into the imprint he had made. I turned my legs so that they were under the table then stood up almost at once as a couple of delegates wandered back through the door into the foyer. One of them stroked the corners of his mouth as though to keep from smiling.

Ike returned a short time later empty-handed.

'I wouldn't look so miserable about it,' I said, sharper than I meant to (the two guys who had just come in were loitering in the background). 'All money in the bank to you, isn't it? I'll pick one up when I get home.'

'You might want to avoid some of the big chains,' he said.

I laughed. 'Spoken like a true Orsola.'

'I'm serious,' he said and for a moment looked it. 'They're only sweetie shops, the half of them.'

The thought seemed to peter out. He had spotted the guys behind me.

'Look, you've still got stuff to do,' I said. He was already past me, already doing it.

As I pulled open the door I clearly heard the word 'Rio', Ike saying, 'No, do you know I've never been.'

It was good and dark now. Out of term-time, and beyond the huddle of conference delegates with their signed copies of *Hurts*, the university appeared abandoned. I remembered with unusual sharpness nights walking across campus when I was a student. I could taste the air practically, feel again the mixture of freedom and fear stirred by the limitlessness of the night sky; feel too the cool, tight embrace of the sheets as I slipped into bed.

I must have shivered.

'Chilly?'

I turned. Tadao was strolling towards me. He had his hooded sweat top zipped up over the conference T-shirt.

'Chillier in Limerick, I would think.'

He nodded, 'Even in the summer.' He dug his hands into his pockets at the memory of it.

'Don't come to Belfast, then,' I said. 'I have friends from down South who say they can never get warm there.'

I noticed a girl standing to one side of him. Or rather, at first, I noticed a hat. A Rasta hat, I would have called it – bouffant crown, short peak – but for its dark camouflage material. The face beneath was small and pale and mostly taken up by a wide, thin-lipped mouth.

'Please excuse me,' said Tadao. 'This is Mami.'

'Mami.' I took her hand. There was no weight in it. Something about it, about her whole physical self, suggested design, not DNA: all bar the purely functional dispensed with. The same could not be said for her dress sense. Working down from the hat, she wore two contrasting neckerchiefs, a sleeveless army surplus jacket, sewing needles ranged like organ pipes along the left lapel, a crocheted skirt, and black and white tights ending in burnt-orange Ugg boots. (Jill had lobbied for a pair the year before last, wore them once and, contrary to the claims made by the ads, hadn't taken them out of the wardrobe since.) Bracelets were backed up as high as her elbows and over one shoulder she carried a dyed red bag, decorated with patch badges: an emergency exit piss-take, with the little green man crashing through glass; a US Army crest with a pair of massive cannabis joints where the olive branch and arrows should be in the eagle's claws.

I asked her had she been at the reading too. She glanced at Tadao.

'Mami doesn't speak English so well.'

'I'm sorry,' I said. 'I have next to no Japanese.'

'English is fine. Just a little slower,' said Tadao. He was trying to see into the foyer where Ike was still talking to the people from Rio.

'How did the photos turn out?' I asked him.

'That is what I wanted to say. There was a problem with my printer. I am going home now to check if it is working.'

'I'm sure it would keep till tomorrow. I mean, all the running you've done already.'

'It's OK,' he said. 'I can drop them in at the hotel.'

He was looking into the foyer again. Mami raised a hand to her mouth and gave the world's smallest cough. The shoulder bag shook, the emergency exit badge curled at one corner, in want of one her needles. Tadao turned to her, apologised in Japanese.

'I'll let him know,' I said. 'I'm sure he'll be delighted.'

Still he hesitated. Mami coughed again.

'OK,' he said, to her, to me, himself maybe.

As they rounded the corner, Mami was trying to work her arm through his – work herself back into the forefront of his mind – bangle by bangle. It could be a long, long process.

They hadn't been gone a minute when Ike came out.

'You just missed Tadao.'

His mouth shaped the name soundlessly, helping his memory out. No light came on.

'This morning? Mount Ogon-zan?'

'Sorry. *Tadao*. I thought you said …'

I rescued him from the lie. 'He's away off to get those photos we took. I told him not to bother his head, but …'

Ike nodded, his thoughts clearly elsewhere.

'So,' I said. 'Rio?'

He manufactured a shrug. 'I don't know. Depends on work.'

'If it was me I wouldn't think twice.'

His eyes slid round to meet mine. I was half expecting him to tell me it wasn't me, was it? But, no, 'You're probably right,' he said.

There was, it seemed, a first time for everything.

He asked me what I had planned now.

'Hotel, I think. Bed.'

'Some of us are going for dinner, if you'd like to come.'

'Dinner?'

'Well I don't know about you, but I didn't eat much at the reception.'

I hadn't done badly myself, but then I could have done a whole lot better.

'It's a wee place Kimiko knows, round the corner from the hotel. You'd be home in five minutes.'

OK, my case was a bit of a mess, but another five or ten minutes would see me packed. He must have seen I was thinking about it.

'Come on ahead. You're a long time dead.'

'As long as you check with Kimiko.'

'I already did.'

'And as long as I can pay my way.'

'Whatever makes you happy.'

'Right then.'

We started walking towards the steps leading down to the road off campus. At the corner I looked back in time to see the lights go out on where we had just been standing. For a second it was as though the place itself had disappeared.

'So, here,' said Ike beside me.

'No,' I interrupted, 'don't say it.'

He didn't, but still the unspoken question hovered about us. When was I going to tell him this story of mine?

dinner

1

There were twelve in the dinner party, not counting me: not counting me, exactly three taxis' worth. When Ike and I arrived at the bottom of the steps, Kimiko was endeavouring simultaneously to guard the three taxis she had booked and secure a fourth, parked immediately behind them. Other delegates prowled around the vehicles, trying doors, tapping the drivers' windows, shouting out destinations, ailments that meant they shouldn't really be standing about at all on cold spring evenings waiting for cabs. The student volunteers were in the thick of it, offering lifts, assuring everyone there were still buses. I caught sight of Tadao and the top of Mami's camouflaged (poorly, as it turned out) Rasta hat. If his car was as accommodating as his nature, I thought, Tadao would have this place cleared in no time.

Ike sized up the situation, muttered something about hanging around here all night, then clutched his flight bag to his chest and barrelled on through to the front.

'Gangway, gangway.'

I followed in his wake, dispensing sorrys, though his passage met with neither resistance nor resentment. He even got a couple of pats on the back on his way through. I got one myself and it was a struggle not to give in to the thought I must have done something to deserve it.

The issue of the fourth car was settled by Ike getting into the back seat. As the honoured guest's guest, I had no option but to get in beside him. A moment later the door opened again and the little man who had made the long announcement about the journal got in behind his own postman's sack of a bag, wedging me in the middle.

'Oof!' he said, as if he was the one being squashed, then leaned across me to introduce himself to Ike. He shook my hand on the way back. Surname Lucas, forename apparently Professor, from *Louvain*. (He pronounced it as though it was open to doubt.)

Kimiko remained on the kerb until all the taxis were filled. At the last minute she pulled Dražen from the one in front of us, to let Klera and Walter Jaufenthaler ride together. Dražen got into the passenger seat of our car and folded his arms.

Ike's hand snaked past me to rest on Dražen's shoulder. 'It's for the greater good,' he said.

'I don't mind,' said Dražen, minding quite a lot, 'but I already move once, to allow Japanese colleagues to be together.'

'"Wanted, conference co-ordinator",' Ike mused. '"Must have background in international diplomacy and marriage guidance counselling."'

Dražen added a third qualification under cover of the taxi engine starting, as Kimiko, who had the directions, climbed into the lead car. Just shy of a hundred pairs of eyes watched us go (among them Olaf Salo's, unreadable behind his glasses), then set their sights on the next batch of taxis making their way up the hill from the expressway.

Ike had retreated into my shadow. Dražen had yet to loosen

the knot he had tied himself in. There being no one else to bother, Lucas asked me had I seen his journal. He showed me a couple of issues, a pale blue and a pale green. Special conference rate: two for the price of one and a half. I told him it was very tempting, but I was flying home in the morning and was already overburdened. He said if I gave him my card he would put me on the mailing list.

'Do you know,' I said. 'I'm right out of cards after that reception tonight.'

We had arrived at the tollbooths back to town. We had in fact been sitting, fourth in the queue of taxis, at our tollbooth for some time already. The attendant was leaning out her window, in heated discussion with the driver of the lead taxi, or her right hand was in heated discussion with his: a pair of irate white glove puppets. Kimiko got out and ran back to our car, clutching a sheet of paper. Dražen got out and for a few moments both their heads were lost to me. Then Dražen ducked back in again.

'I think you should look at this,' he said.

The doors opened on either side of me. Lucas exited left, Ike right. I sat tight. Urgent conference business obviously. No concern of mine.

A horn sounded behind us. Our driver wound down his window, joined in the puppetry. Kimiko had gone to talk in the windows of the other two taxis. It didn't look like we were moving any time soon. I slid across to the open door on my left.

'What's the problem?'

Ike was holding the paper now. A4, crosshatched with folds. It couldn't have been bigger than a book of matches before it was opened out and even now seemed to want to close in on itself. The writing, though, was bold as brass. I could make it out from behind and in reverse.

'Not Long Left.'

'Where did that come from?' I asked and Kimiko, talking to

someone in the car ahead, not to me, said, 'I was opening my bag to look for my cell phone and there it was. But I had had the bag open only a short time before, when we were waiting for the taxis to arrive. I would have noticed it, I am certain.'

The other three people in her taxi were City University bods. It was inconceivable that they were responsible, and anyway Kimiko had been in the front seat, with the bag on her lap. The note must have been put there in the scrum to get into the taxi.

'But there were so many people,' Dražen said. 'It could have been anybody.'

'It could have been you,' said Ike. For the first time Dražen's look was not that of a friend. 'Or me, putting the wind up people.'

'But why would you?' Kimiko had rejoined them. She couldn't have sounded more hurt if Ike had in fact confessed.

'Sick sense of humour, sour grapes … There are over a hundred delegates at this conference. We shouldn't be surprised if there's one head-case in amongst them. It's the law of averages.'

The attendant had now left the tollbooth. She had given up remonstrating with the taxi driver and was instead trying to stop any more traffic coming into our lane. One of her colleagues was on the phone, glancing out his booth at us.

'We will have the authorities here again in a minute if we are not careful,' said Lucas.

Kimiko took the note back. Her hand was shaking. 'I think we should go somewhere else to eat.'

'You're not serious,' said Ike.

'It might be safer. Too many people know which izakaya we are going to.'

'No,' Ike said firmly. 'We'll go where we were planning to go. Dražen, help me out here.'

Dražen mumbled it didn't matter to him either way, as long as everyone was … Ike cut across him, appealing to me. 'Tell them,' he said.

'What?' I asked. Even the people in the other taxis appeared to be looking at me, though they couldn't possibly be following all this.

'What it used to be like at home. What we did when things were really bad.'

'What?' I asked again. Same word, different question. When things were *really* bad?

'We went out, didn't we? Same as always. It's the only way.'

One of the university bods had got out of the lead taxi. His hair, in the super wattage of the tollbooth lights, pure silver. He spoke urgently to Kimiko.

'The taxi driver says he will leave without us,' she translated.

'So?' Ike asked.

Kimiko folded the page carefully and placed it in her pocket. 'So –' her mouth made a small smile – 'we'll go where we said we would.'

Dražen shrugged. As long as everyone was happy …

No one was happier than the attendant as she walked back along the line to her booth. She nodded emphatically as each taxi passed through, her index finger like a log rolling: Go, go, go, *go*.

In the tunnel I apologised to Ike for my apparent lack of support.

'You know, I was standing there thinking, *What did we do?* And then I realised, I never really was a young man there, going out all the time, I mean, not when it was, like, completely mental. I went straight from school to university across the water. I came back a married man with children.'

We were out of the tunnel, crossing the bridge, and with an odd tilt of the imagination I saw us briefly from above, eagle-eye view, a metal projectile speeding along a lane towards the flashing lights and random sounds of Hiroshima city centre.

'Did you never think of getting out yourself?' I asked.

Ike spoke to his own reflection. 'A couple of times, I did.'

'Thought about it?'

'Got out.'

'When?'

He opened his hands in a gesture of precision taking flight. 'The seventies.'

'Oh.'

I would have said more – what about that passage he had read? – had he not suddenly sat forward to talk to Dražen at the same moment as Lucas, on the other side of me, tapped my wrist. Did I have much contact with bookshops at home? Only he was looking into the possibility of five-colour covers for his journal and … And we were back in the city now. I let him witter on at me while I trained all but one ear on the world outside the car windows.

'Right,' I said, every now and then, the word as remote as a light programmed to come on when you're out, to fool would-be intruders. 'Right.'

For the second time already today I had the curious sensation of sobering up when I wasn't even aware I had been tipsy. Really, I'd had next to nothing at the reception; but then I had never been much of a drinker. Two or three, that was usually my limit. Even after a quarter-century's practice, I could still be poleaxed by one. Like the one I had – how many days ago now? – in the hotel's Skylight bar. White wine, enormous measure, closer to a bucket than a glass. I hadn't been able to sit in the roof garden because of the renovations, so I contented myself with a table beside one of the floor-to-ceiling windows, which was probably where that idea just now of the city as giant pinball table had come from, though my main memory was of playing games of Connect Four with the lighted windows of the downtown office blocks. Only twenty-five floors up and already the city was a toyshop. Imagine from thirty-one thousand feet how it looked. A huff and a puff …

Not that thoughts like this seemed to bother any of the other drinkers. They were mostly young Japanese down at this end of the room, away from the restaurant. Their drinks were electric blue and shocking pink. (Once the decor was sorted out someone would have to get to work on the cocktail menu.) There were a lot of photographs being taken. A lot of *chisu* and peace signs. Clearly to be up here was to have arrived somewhere.

The bucket of wine was well over a fiver, the peanuts the guts of three pounds a bowl, but I could see the attraction of sitting all night, allowing yourself to become nicely stewed. A diagram of a runway was sketched in bright green lights on the outer rim of the city. After a time other lights ascended from it into the sky, a white pair flanked by a red, dimming by degrees, disappearing. The last plane of the day out of Hiroshima regional.

I was still looking off in that direction when I saw the handprint splayed on the window. It was about two feet off the floor, just above my knee. I brushed against it with my trouser leg and when that didn't work leaned over to give it a quick wipe with my napkin. No effect whatever. I wiped again, harder, though by now I had twigged – the hand was on the outside of the glass. A waiter stopped by my table, asked was everything OK.

'Yes.' I sat up too quickly, lost his face in a whirl of stars. 'Everything's fine.'

He picked up the lacquered bowl the nuts had been in. I waited a moment after he had gone then looked down, through the glass, through the handprint's improbable high-five, till the remaining stars faded like the lights of the last plane out.

2

I had lost sight of where we were for a while in the turns the taxi was taking. The lights of the Hana's Skylight bar came briefly into view as our cavalcade passed along the front of the Peace Park, then were eclipsed as we turned left, just over the bridge, into a narrow street open on one side to the river and the park's east face. Despite the chill, the picnickers were out in force on both banks of the river. Hanami was not a fair weather affair. Some had brought rugs to spread on the ground, glasses, bowls, little stoves to cook on; most sat on the blue mats I had seen for sale earlier outside the convenience store, drinking beer from plastic cups, passing round giant bags of crisps.

We pulled in above the landing stage for the passenger boats that plied the river in daylight hours. There was a little open-air café here too during the day, but now the shutters were up, the umbrellas down, and the only food on offer was from an Octopus Ball stall at the foot of Motoyasu Bridge. The bridge itself was a meeting point for waifs and strays, night as well as day: guitar strummers, hair braiders. They might have been employed to sit there cross-legged, endlessly rolling their cigarettes, so much a part of the whole Peace Park scheme did they seem. Even so, I sensed that a few of our party were eyeing them warily as the taxis drove away, leaving us on the kerbside: the aftereffects of the note in Kimiko's bag. That was one thing I did remember from the not-so-good old days at home, the difficulty deciding whether you were safer in a bunch, or simply a bigger target.

'It is just across the road,' said Kimiko and for a moment I thought she was referring to the elegant-looking café-bar on the corner to our left. But no.

The place we were going to was facing that, the pretty nondescript ground floor of a typically featureless fill-in building on what, sixty years ago, had been the most comprehensively scorched earth on earth. There were vending machines either side of the entrance, a green pay phone on a stand, its flex leading back through a gap in one of the double sliding doors. On this side too there was a pair of posters, one above the other, of a young woman with a large tankard of Kirin. In the top picture she was wearing a pink kimono; in the bottom, a turquoise blouse and white cardigan. For the Japanese woman you are, they seemed to say, though clearly not to the Mamis of this town, or the girls on Motoyasu Bridge.

Below the posters a silver and black motor scooter had been parked, an empty yellow crate strapped to the rack on its rear mudguard.

I got the feeling that even a few of our Japanese hosts were underwhelmed. Kimiko, however, had recovered her enthusiasm since the discussion at the tollbooth.

'This is a most excellent izakaya,' she said and stepped around the pay phone to slide back the door on a gas heater, balancing, alarmingly, on polystyrene blocks dead in the centre of the floor. 'Most excellent.'

If she had said most unexpected, I couldn't have argued. Wherever you looked, higher than the heater, there were flowers, in roughly cast pots and elegant vases, on the counter, on the tables, on cardboard boxes: daisies and lilies and roses and freesias and big, blousy chrysanthemums. There were flowers in the still-lives hung in gilt frames about the walls, flowers on the plastic apron of the woman who greeted us from behind the bar as though we were the last of her relatives arrived for the festivities. The curtain across the cupboard above her head was so old, or unwashed, it looked like hide, but even then the eye was drawn to the stem of japonica laid on top, as though in atonement to the god of hygiene.

Two women sat at the counter with glasses of beer, but otherwise the customers were men. They all seemed to be speaking at once, all seemed to be speaking to our party, which was gathered now around the gas heater. They were half-cut the lot of them. There was some banter with Kimiko, who pointed to each of the Europeans in turn, naming our country of origin: *kuroachia, o-sutoria* ... Several of the customers stood up and bowed as each was mentioned, the others raised their glasses ... *airurando.*

The cry went up, '*Airurando?*'

Yes, Kimiko said, Ireland, and was turning to say something particular about Ike when one of the men who had been bowing linked his hands wide to the right of his shoulder, then swung them, hard.

'*Gorufu!*'

Everyone joined in the laughter, or at least everyone whose face I could see. I was standing just behind Ike. I leaned closer.

'There's an idea for the next book, *My Struggle: An Irish Golfer's Handicap.*'

His shoulders twitched. If it was a laugh it was a fleeting one. Never mind, I made a mental note for future U-bag information packs: stick in something about Royal Portrush or at the very least a photograph of Darren Clarke.

A second woman wearing a flowered apron, in her fifties like the first and like her with something of the fifties French film star about her clothes and hair, now approached and walked us to the rear of the bar. Steps on the left led to a dining area with low tables and cushions on tatami mats. More flower prints, more vases, and – a new touch here – wall clocks of various shapes and sizes proclaiming as wide a variety of times. I wondered was this for the benefit of lunching businessmen and remembered the clocks I had seen in the JETRO office, which if I had my bearings right was just a short walk from here. Five clocks there, showing the Hiroshima hour in New York, London, Sydney, Bombay. Dear knows what minute they were showing, for, as here, no two minute-hands agreed.

Kimiko wanted to know were we all happy to eat in this fashion, though of course the truth was that most visitors, having prepared themselves to expect it, were put out to discover that eating in this fashion was not the norm. We shuffled out of our shoes, some with more cause to be self-conscious than others (I was doubly glad now I had made it back to the hotel for that shower). I stood behind Dražen on the steps, waiting while the seating was being worked out. There was a hole in one of his socks through which the middle toe would poke, then withdraw, then poke again: caught in a bad toe-dream, naked when all around were dressed.

The upshot of all the seat arranging was (surprise, surprise) a table divided, right end, left end, between Japanese and non-Japanese, with Kimiko, forever the facilitator, plonked in the middle. She explained to those at our end, on behalf of those at the other, that we were being honoured with the better view, which in my case, having been the last seated, after Lucas, two places down on the opposite side from Ike, amounted to a railway station clock, showing twenty-five to four, and the door out to the toilets.

There were no menus. Kimiko asked would we permit her to order. We permitted. The woman who had shown us to our table returned without a notepad and knelt while Kimiko spoke to her. She seemed from her gestures to be describing a mood more than a meal. The waitress chipped in with a few words and gestures of her own, as though to confirm they had the same thing in mind. Kimiko waved a hand to erase one false impression, corroborated the rest with nods then smiles. One of her male colleagues introduced a late amendment. Kimiko gave him to understand it was a stroke of genius, that all her ordering had merely been circling the subject, but his had got to the very heart of it. Or maybe I was reading too much into her gushing delivery. When the waitress had left, with a bow to seal the agreement, Kimiko turned to our end of the table again.

'In this izakaya, they serve only what is fresh and in season,' she said, 'and only this type of beer.'

There were four litre-bottles of Kirin on the table, skyscrapers next to the low-rise tumblers. Kimiko lifted the bottle nearest her by the neck and base.

'In Japan, you know, it is the custom to serve your neighbour and not yourself.'

In Japan, so far as I could tell, it was the custom to repeat that this was the custom before every meal.

Kimiko poured beer into half a dozen glasses, explaining as she did, as someone always did, that we had to keep hold of our glass while it was being filled and that if we were not ready for more when it was offered we had simply to place a hand over the top. She set the bottle down and looked at the table. I reacted fastest, picking up the bottle and filling a seventh glass for her. She looked up again and smiled at me: the first time. Someone had already taken care of the drinks to her right.

'So,' she said and we all raised our glasses. '*Kanpai!*'

'*Santé!*'

'*Prosit!*'

'*Živjeli!*'

'*Sláinte!*'

'Cheers!'

Ike leaned across the table to me. 'This is where it starts to get messy.' Food arrived. Oden – hotpot: tofu, silken and fried, daikon and potato, boiled egg, fish cake, balls of sticky rice.

Kimiko suggested sake. Flasks were brought warm to the table. She served Ike and Dražen and Lucas and Klera and Walter and me. Dražen served Kimiko.

Kanpai! Santé! Prosit! Živjeli! Sláinte! Cheers!

We filled our bowls with hotpot, ate in silence, then, as one, made sounds of approval. This was *good*. Kimiko smiled. The secret was in the cooking time – the longer the better – and the stock. The cook here would have his own recipe. We had another drink to toast him.

Dražen served Ike, Lucas, Klera, Walter, Kimiko and me. I served Dražen.

Kanpai! Santé! Prosit! Živjeli! Sláinte! Cheers!

We ate more. Nodded our satisfaction to the other end of the table. Drank more.

Lucas served Dražen and Ike and Klera and Walter and Kimiko and me. Walter served Lucas.

Kanpai! Santé! Prosit! Živjeli! Sláinte! Cheers!

The oden pots were taken away. Plates were brought: broad beans, baby leeks in a yellow sauce. 'Very delicious,' Kimiko assured us and was not wrong. More Kirin came, more sake.

I served sake to Kimiko and Klera and Lucas and Ike, beer to Dražen and Walter. Kimiko served sake to me.

Kanpai! Santé! Prosit! Živjeli! Sláinte! Cheers!

Ike got up and went to the toilet. Lucas started talking about his journal. Dražen told him, 'Not while we are eating', then in case he had hurt his feelings, topped up his glass with sake. He topped up Klera, Walter and me. Kimiko placed her hand over her glass. Klera topped up Dražen.

Santé! Prosit! Živjeli! Cheers!

The broad bean and leek plates had been picked clean. The waitress took them away. Ike returned; Lucas departed. Klera noticed Ike was empty. She served him sake. She served me.

Kimiko had her hand on her glass. Klera served beer to Walter and Dražen. Walter went to serve her. 'No,' she said, but too late. She inflated her cheeks, blew air out slowly. We raised our glasses in encouragement.

Prosit! Živjeli! Sláinte! Cheers!

Lucas returned. His hair was combed. 'Your hair is combed,' Dražen said. 'It is not,' said Lucas.

The waitress brought plates of fish, barbecued five to a wooden skewer. Our end of the table wondered what they were. '*Eto-ne, koiwashi.*' Kimiko couldn't remember the word in English. She consulted with the other end, came back with 'small sardine'.

'You mean like anchovy?' I said.

She consulted again. No, small sardine. Anchovy was another word: *katakuchiiwashi.*

'*Katakuchiiwashi!*', six voices repeated. We had to drink to that. With beer in my left hand, sake in my right, I served Lucas and Dražen and Klera and Walter and Ike. Kimiko took her hand from her glass. I served her. She served me.

Katakuchiiwashi!

Kanpai! Santé! Prosit! Živjeli! Sláinte! Cheers!

I was already way past my usual limit, but, maybe it was the food (I had had a whole boiled egg from the oden), the drink was going down like it was lemonade: nothing worse than a burp or two to stifle.

Klera went to the toilet. A moment later Dražen went, followed by Walter's eyes. More small sardines were requested. More small sardines were brought. Dražen came back from the toilet, talking of roses: on the sill above the urinal, had we seen? Such a red. His father grew roses. There was a red he had, Ingrid Bergman, exactly like the one above the urinal.

His eyes were shining.

Ike, lo and behold, reached for the sake and served him, then Kimiko, then Lucas, then me. Walter had his hand on his glass, his eyes still on the toilet door.

Ingrid Bergman!

Kanpai! Santé! Živjeli! Sláinte! Cheers!

Walter went to the toilet. The plates with the skewers were taken away and replaced by plates of *koiwashi* in their uncooked state, filleted, with mackerel, octopus and squid.

I asked about the order of the dishes: raw fish after cooked. Kimiko shrugged, entirely at her ease now. 'There isn't a *law*,' she said, as though amazed that anyone would think that the precise sequence of dishes, unlike the precise seating of guests, the precise more or less everything you cared to name, should be subject to ritual.

We drank to it anyway, no-law.

Dražen served Kimiko and Ike and me. Lucas kept his hand on his glass. Kimiko served Dražen.

Kanpai! Živjeli! Sláinte! Cheers!

We threw in a *prosit* too this time for the absent Jaufenthalers, who returned almost at once, arm in arm. Klera covered her mouth with her fingertips.

'There is no ladies,' she said, 'just a door through the room where the men stand. There was no one there when I went in, but then … one after the other, they came. I couldn't leave.'

Kimiko said no one would have minded. Klera said she heard a certain man talking to himself. She looked at Dražen. He didn't blush. To the *roses*, he said, and we took that for a toast and emptied our glasses.

Walter served Klera and Kimiko and Dražen and Ike and me. Lucas kept his glass covered with both hands. Klera served Walter.

Kanpai! Prosit! Živjeli! Sláinte! Cheers!

Dražen said *sláinte* in Croatian was 'small elephant'. I choked, spluttered, jumped up with sake all down me. Kimiko quickly explained to the other end of the table. Their worried expressions creased with laughter. Up went the glasses, even Lucas's, though it went down again without a drop being drunk.

Small elephants!

The fish was eaten. The plates were taken. The bottles remained. The glasses were filled and emptied and refilled. The toasts were called, small elephants, every time. We served each other and were served in our turn, all except Lucas, whose head at times was almost on top of the hand on his glass. Once, Ike poured sake over my hand, so surprised was he to find it in the way; once, I forgot and served myself, then tried to drink away the mistake while filling the glasses around me.

Small elephants!

3

I looked at my watch one moment and it was a quarter to ten, looked again and it was half past. The railway station clock by the toilet doors still showed twenty-five to four. I glanced at the other clocks off and on for a few minutes. Not one moved. Now I no longer thought of the JETRO office, but of the museum, as far again in the opposite direction across Motoyasu Bridge. I imagined these clocks being bought stopped, like sculptures of individual moments, windows on to worlds where eight-fifteen had never been.

I looked at my watch again. Five to eleven. I should have left long ago. I was sober enough to know I was drunk, drunk enough to kid myself another half-hour would make no difference now.

Ike was talking about a place he had been to in Tokyo, the Bitter End. Wasn't that a great name? he asked us. He was going to write a book set in Tokyo and call it *The Bitter End*.

'How long were you in Tokyo?' I asked.

He didn't even turn to dismiss the criticism implied. 'Oh for God's sake. I didn't say a *guide*-book.'

'Right,' I said then lost track of the conversation for a while, my ear tuned inwards. Something he had said was niggling. I cast about; caught it. 'Why bitter?' He turned this time. His face was his question. *What?*

'That's all you ever hear, the *bitter* end. Makes you wonder, is there no other sort.' I was picking at the label of a Kirin bottle, my fingernails making the connection: only one type of beer here, only one end ahead of us. 'I mean – is that the best we can hope for?'

Ike's lip curled, his mouth opened, but it was Lucas, raising his head, who said, 'It is a different word. *Bitter*. It is to do with boats. Or maybe ropes. I read it somewhere.' He was flagging again. 'A journal.'

Ike had occupied his open mouth with a drink. When he took the glass away his lip had straightened out.

'Boats *and* ropes,' he said. 'The bitts are what you dangle your anchor from.'

'Ah.'

'So you see,' Dražen said, 'there is hope after all.'

And we did small elephants to that too: an end without bitterness.

'Or ropes,' I added. 'Or ropes,' they said.

For a moment then there was silence on either side of Kimiko. It seemed as though we might have arrived at an end ourselves. Then Ike struck his thigh.

'But, anyway, I was telling you, this other bar I was in, last time I was here, in Kobe, near one of the ferry terminals.' It seemed I had been absent from the conversation for longer than I had imagined. 'A bit hole-and-corner, but a friend of a friend of the British Council guy I was with had recommended it.'

'The Freshest Sashimi You'll Ever Eat,' I said.

He nodded, letting his eyes close to keep sight of what he was going to say next. 'I think the friend, or the friend's friend, was to meet us, but one thing and another, there we are sitting at the bar, just the two of us. The British Council guy, he has the basics, so we're not stuck. We're having a couple of drinks, a wee bit of this and that to eat, getting a few looks, but nothing we haven't had before in other places we've been. Next thing this fella has hopped up on a stool beside us, wants to know what part of America we're from. Chatty enough, like, so your man from the Council – what's this you called him? It'll come to me. Anyway, your man, he explains we're not Americans: he's from England, I'm from Northern Ireland. There's a few people listening in around the bar by now, like. They murmur a bit at this, I don't think they like the sound of Northern Ireland at all, but the fella that's talking to us, he seems to move in even closer.'

I started to get a terrible sense of déjà vu, which only got worse for me naming it and only faded when I tried to pin it to a source. Not this morning's dream, at least. But still the feeling lingered that I had been somewhere very like this before.

'The British Council guy ... Victor. That's what you call him. Victor tells the fella I'm a writer and the fella comes in closer still. A writer! He wants to buy us a drink and then, of course, Victor has to buy him one back and then I'm thinking, right, that's us, lovely meeting you and all ... But your man says, hold on, I want you to have something, and he calls over the barman and he talks away to him, and the next thing there's a bottle of sake this big' – hands two feet apart – 'being set up on the counter. So I'm saying to Victor, look, tell him thanks, but really we have to be going, and he turns round and repeats all this, and then the fella says something back, and Victor turns to me again. It's not to drink here, he says. It's a present.'

Ike paused for another drink. 'What's this now he said it was? Nada-something.'

'Nada No Ki-ippon,' said several people at once. There was respect in their voices.

'That's the stuff. Nada No ...'

'Ki-ippon.'

'Right. So, of course, we had to buy one more drink to thank him, one more drink for all his friends standing around earwigging – luckily enough Victor had money on him – and then we said, seriously, time we were making a move, but the fella still won't hear of it. Wait, he says, one more thing, and he calls over the barman and has another long talk and away the barman goes, down the bar, and lifts down this wooden block thing from a shelf and sets it on the counter in front of me. You know the things I mean? They've got characters – writing – on them.'

'I think this is an ornament made to resemble a Shogi piece,' said Kimiko. 'Japanese chess.'

Ike nodded, pressed on: 'Here's me to Victor, listen, if that's for me, tell him, really, I can't take it. I mean, it's too much, but also, the size of it ...' He measured off something about half the size of the sake bottle, gabled at the top. 'I'm talking solid wood.'

'Yes,' said Kimiko, 'this is a Shogi piece.'

'There was no way I wanted to be lugging that all the way home with me. Anyway, I didn't know if it was his to give. He hadn't offered the barman any money and he didn't *look* like he owned the place. But he kept on insisting, take it, take it. He was pointing to the character cut into the wood. Victor translated. It means luck, he said. The symbol for horse, reversed. I wasn't really looking at it. I was looking at the fella's finger. There was a bit missing from the end.'

All around the table the word was whispered: 'Yakuza'. I whispered it myself. My firm's head of security had briefed me before I left Belfast.

'Exactly,' Ike said. 'Victor was prodding me in the back, like, just pick the thing up and let's go, but just as I was about to lay hold of it your man's hand shoots out and clamps on to my wrist. I swear you could hardly have made one decent finger out of the bits and pieces he had. And here he is: You will have good fortune as long as you keep this by your desk, but – he squeezed my wrist; even without the fingers he had some grip – but if you ever return to Japan and don't come back to this bar, *your luck will run out.*'

He had become the Kobe Yakuza, we had become Ike leaning in to catch the last five barely whispered words. He clapped his hands, laughing, and sat back. We all sat back too. Jumped.

'That's a lot of bunk,' I blurted, surprised at my bluntness, but thankful that the first word I had reached for had eluded me. Not infringement. *Plagiarism.* The more he had talked the more I was sure I knew this story.

'Cross my heart and hope to die,' he said, the playground pledge, nailed down with a forefinger on the right nipple. 'As soon as we were out the door, me and Victor started running … well, staggering fast, with all that stuff we had to carry. We dived into the first taxi we saw. Victor told me the fella at the bar had started saying something about a sword he wanted me to have. It was like, I don't know, someone coming to Belfast and popping in for a light bite in a UVF bar: Hold on there till I get you a wee home-made machine gun to take back with you.'

More explanations further down the table. More smiles. I felt the Japanese listeners were quietly impressed by this casual reference to paramilitary armaments.

'*Now,*' I said, trusting that they, and Ike, would hear in that one word how unlikely it was that anything of the kind would ever befall a visitor to our city. The phantom-club swinger earlier was more right than he, or they, knew: you were probably in greater danger these days from a flying golf ball than a gun.

The word fell, the ears were deaf.

'Excuse me for asking,' said Kimiko, 'but did you go back to the bar on this trip?'

Ike laughed louder. 'Are you mad? I was lucky enough to get out the last time. The fella was a lunatic. I wouldn't go back if you paid me.'

'And you are not worried about your luck?'

He shook his head. He had anticipated this question, might even have been depending on it. 'It was a bit of wood the man gave me. Beautiful and everything, but a bit of wood all the same. You make your own luck in this business. Like when I got home, I could have set the thing up on my desk, given it a wee rub every time I sat down to write and fat lot of good it would have done me. But you know what I did? I wrote a piece for the papers – *Sunday Times* – word for word what I just told you. As a friend of mine says, use everything but the squeal. The back-to-front horse has nothing to do with it. It's knowing a good story when you find one.'

That's where I'd heard it before. Read it.

'Was that you?' I said. 'About two or three years ago?'

'Nearly four.'

'A whole big spread?' I was the world's worst for remembering names, *noticing* them, half the time.

The heads at the far end of the table had come together in muffled consternation. They parted just as Kimiko recited, '"You will be sorry for what you wrote."'

The heads nodded.

'Oh, come on, now,' Ike said. 'You're not seriously telling me you think the Yakuza were combing the Sunday colour supplements to see what I would say about them and *then* waited nearly four years to pay me back?'

The expressions said that was exactly what they did think. Next thing, I felt like telling him, they'll be thinking you can score yourself a machine gun over lunch in a Belfast bar.

'"You know who you are",' Kimiko said, then, more ominously still, '"Not long left".'

The door to the toilets opened, as the door to the toilets had been opening ever since we sat down, but, as though the repetition of the words had renewed the threat, all heads turned towards it: one businessman leaned a heavy hand on the shoulder of another, making sure he didn't walk out on the end of the joke. We couldn't have been further from their fuddled minds.

The waitress reappeared. All heads turned from the businessmen to her. All heads shook at the offer of green tea. Watches were being consulted, phones produced. They had been fortunate up to now, why push their luck a minute further?

Kimiko slipped away, clutching her bag. I slipped away behind her while Ike cajoled the table into relaxing, having another drink, *not being ridiculous.* I caught up with her by the till, under the leaves of a large rubber plant.

'Please,' I said, producing my gold card. 'Let me get part of this.'

She shook her head, turned back to the till, where there having been no order as such there was now no bill. She and the waitress talked it out between them.

'The drinks, even,' I said into a lull.

'You are our guest,' said Kimiko.

'I am already grateful. I got to meet the mayor. Besides I can claim all this back as expenses. At least let me pay for my own.'

'One-thirteenth portion,' she said. 'It is not much.'

'Let me get everyone a liqueur,' I said.

Kimiko was bending to sign the credit card slip. Her hair fell forward and she had to tuck the loose strands behind her ear to keep them out of her eyes. She looked tired all of a sudden, of me, of conference organising, I didn't know. She spoke wearily to the waitress who returned with us to the table.

'Whiskey anyone?' I asked. 'Brandy?'

Ike's face lit up, less, I guessed, at the prospect of more drink than at the thought that by proposing it I was siding with him.

'Good man yourself,' he said as I took my place again, his voice the sole bright note in the general gloom.

Dražen, opposite him, supposed if there was something along the lines of *cherry* brandy ...

Kimiko asked, the waitress thought, then said, yes, she believed there was. Dražen rallied and the tide turned. One by one the rest of them named their poison. Even Lucas agreed to have a little something, though he looked truly sorry that he had ever agreed to edit a journal, let alone one so successful that he got invited along to dinners like this. Maybe the five-colour covers could keep a while yet.

I didn't want to think too much myself about how I was going to feel. This was no time to be adding to the cocktail of drinks I had drunk. The bar was already half empty when I was round at the till. Even people without planes to catch in the morning were turning their thoughts to bed.

The drinks arrived, carried by the two waitresses. Seeing the women side by side for the first time, it was hard not to be struck by the similarity, the accuracy of their period mimicry. They might have been under the influence of one of the stopped clocks. No bomb, but no mobile phones either, with or without internet access. No internet, come to that. Barely even stage one of the food-wrap revolution.

They knelt to distribute the drinks, some of which, they said through Kimiko, came from bottles they had never opened in all their years here. (Nell flashed into my mind, standing at the sink emptying Camp Coffee down the plughole.) Most of their customers had their own bottles of sake behind the counter. Serving was just a question of decanting a flask from one of them or flipping the cap on another bottle of Kirin. They had sunk back a little on their heels, settling themselves for a good old chat. How many visitors to this part of town, after all, faced with the open aspect of the café across the street and the obstacle course in front of this place ever chose the latter?

From the way our crowd were reaching for their glasses, however, they seemed to want to throw the drinks back and have done. *Finito.* Good night. Then Ike, using Lucas's shoulder for leverage, got to his feet, staying their hands. The black suit looked none the worse for another day's wear.

'I just wanted to thank Kimiko for arranging this dinner here tonight, to thank our wonderful hosts …' The waitresses' first instinct was to look over their shoulders to see who his bow had really been aimed at; their second, seeing no one, was to tilt their heads and titter. 'To thank all of you for your company, and, finally, to say ... safe home now.'

He raised his glass, making 'safe home now' sound like a toast, not the taunt that I knew damn well it was. There was a moment's hesitation while we huddled masses waited for him to return to our level, then we were all on our feet.

'Safe home now,' we solemnly chorused, or rather, they did. 'Small elephants,' I said, into my twelve-year-old Suntory, and then drained it.

Christ Almighty.

'OK!' Ike's voice lanced the roar in my ears. 'Who's in for the third party?'

third party

1

When all the excuses had been made, goodbyes had been said, there were four of us on the pavement before the izakaya: Dražen, Kimiko, Ike and me. Not even Klera and Walter could be persuaded to join us.

'Fuck them,' Ike said.

'Where to?' I said. 'Hotel bar?'

'Fuck that,' said Ike, man of four letters.

'Where then?'

'Naga–, Naga–.' he clicked his fingers to conjure the rest of the word, or else keep it from running into the name of the Kobe sake.

'Nagarekawa,' Kimiko said.

'Very spot.'

I knew the district, though for the most part I had given it a wide berth after dark: a second, more discreet briefing before leaving Belfast; too many little nooks and crannies, too many places in among the grub and club signs for the unwary to go astray. By day the streets had an almost religious cast: every other shop, it seemed, a Buddhist home-supply store; by night they were the province of spivvy youths with long dyed hair and ill-fitting double-breasted suits, girls carrying menus with photos of still more girls, scoping the crowds for American servicemen.

'We talking taxi?' I asked.

Ike scoffed. 'Listen to you, *taxi*.'

Dražen was stamping his foot on the pavement. 'My leg has gone to sleep.'

'Walking's the best thing for it,' said Ike.

'It is only five minutes,' Kimiko said.

'Come on, then.' Ike led off.

Kimiko caught him by the shoulders. 'This way,' she said and about-faced him.

Almost at once we were under cover of Hondori Arcade, all but empty at this end and at this hour. Our voices, with little to absorb them, came back at us from the high roof. They sounded like they had got a second wind from somewhere. I began to feel a bit breezier myself. What was that sign they used to have over the door of our conference room at work? 'Do something every day you have never done before.' I had been to bars after dinner countless times in my life, but I had never been to a 'third party'. It had a ring, even if Kimiko was in two minds about whether the reception earlier counted as a *first* party. We broke cover briefly to stand at a pedestrian crossing the width of a half-decent football pitch. A bus passed on its way to the third floor of Sogo. I opened my mouth to say, Wait till I tell you what happened to me today, then shut it again. The traffic lights changed. A couple of schoolboys overtook us on their bikes, their daylong relay far from run.

There was only one star above us: a torch bulb throwing a big white moon on to the navy blue sheet of the sky. We crossed over. The torch bulb went out, the arcade lights came on again.

I was on familiar ground here. I had bid a mental farewell to these same shop fronts all of six hours ago on my way back to the hotel with the handbag for my wife. And down one of these side streets was the cocktail bar I had gone to with Haraguchi-san, the evening of our visit to the A-Bomb Museum. Funny how cities shrink with use. Then it had felt as though we had walked Hiroshima to its last letter. Though I *did* have Haraguchi-san for company. He told me a lot about old Hondori as we walked, or at least read it to me, from the booklet on old Hondori I had bought in the museum.

A blue bin lorry was coming down the arcade towards us, crewed by a smiling couple who looked as if they had taken up rubbish collection as a retirement hobby. They stopped outside the chemist of the never-ending Wham!, picked up a few neatly trussed specimens and continued on their way. Both the lorry and the arcade in its wake were spotless. I felt like applauding, it was all so uncomplicated. I felt like telling every Japanese person I passed they were never to take their blue bin lorries for granted.

We were nearing the end of Hondori, where the street split left and right on the prow of the Parco department store. We drifted to the right. The window-dressers had moved in. They had pulled half a dozen mannequins on to the street while they worked on the backdrop, a city skyline made out of soft-drink cans. The mannequins had neither clothes nor heads, but managed to suggest by their postures that even with heads on they would not have seen eye to eye.

Ike performed an elaborate bow before them. 'Allow me to introduce you: Headless meet Legless.'

'Legless?' Kimiko asked. I thought there was an edge to her voice.

'He means drunk,' I said.

'Oh.'

It occurred to me she might have taken it as a dig at Dražen.

'How is your foot?' I asked him.

'I cannot feel my toes.'

'That reminds me of a man I knew,' I said. 'Went to the doctor complaining he had no sensation in his right hand.'

'This is a joke, right?' Ike said.

I ignored him. 'So the doctor looked at it and do you know what he said?'

'What?' said Dražen.

'Don't ask him, it's a joke.'

'The doctor said, you're right, it's an unsensational hand.'

'Listen to him, he thinks he's funny,' said Ike. 'Don't you? You think you're funny.'

'I don't understand,' said Dražen.

'It wouldn't be any funnier if you did,' Ike said. 'Believe me.'

I smiled to myself. I had another one I had come up with on the plane, about the fella who applied to join the mile-high club: solo membership. But perhaps I would save that for later.

Someone called out Kimiko's name: a woman in a red dress, waving from a first-floor balcony across from Parco. Bar-lights shone, bright, behind her. Kimiko squinted, then waved back.

'Friend of yours?' Ike asked.

'An opera singer, very famous, once upon a time.'

Each of us must have assumed that another would ask the obvious question. None of us did, though I noticed, as we turned down towards the okonomiyaki village, Ike sneak a backward glance at the woman. The worst words a writer could hear, used that way: *once upon a time*. Looking over it all, that was the moment when I began to understand him.

Sated okonomiyaki patrons were leaving the tower block where I had eaten last night. Kimiko was anxious to know had I sampled the local 'delicacy'. I assured her that I had.

'So?' Her face was a picture of expectation.

'Interesting,' I said.

Expectation gave way to disappointment.

'No, really, it was. Very interesting.'

'Visitors usually tell me it is very delicious.'

'I wrote to a colleague about it,' I said, and she nodded that this was indeed its due.

A trio of vintage American cars were parked along one side of the narrow street: monstrous gas-guzzlers, so wide, and sitting so low on their suspensions, it was difficult to imagine they had been driven there; lowered in by crane seemed more likely. Young men in vintage Levis milled around them, checking out the chrome work, the upholstery, or whatever it is young men in vintage Levis look at in vintage American cars, the young women in the passenger seats excepted. (I was a confirmed Citroën driver. From 2CV to Xsara, I had only ever had eyes for the next rung up the comfort ladder.)

We came out on to Chuo-dori: Central Avenue; bicycles parked half a dozen deep against a barrier to our left. Nagarekawa began behind the buildings opposite. Before them a long line of taxis prowled, the one in front never quite coming to a halt before its rear door opened and it snaffled a reveller who had staggered out of a side street and strayed too near to the kerb. It was an unfair contest. It was halfway to feeding frenzy.

Ike and the others had already started across the road.

'Thanks for waiting,' I said when I finally caught up with them. There were magnolias in bloom along the kerbside: old lady flowers, I had always thought, but positively revolutionary-looking amid all the cherry blossom.

'No time for dallying,' Ike said. He was reading a hinged blackboard before a wide, open vestibule. I looked at it over his shoulder.

'No!' I said. 'It's my last drink in Hiroshima. Not in here.'

Like 'Northern' and 'Ireland' on a book cover, there were no words I dreaded more to see paired on a blackboard than 'Irish' and 'Bar'.

'Kimiko wants to go in,' Ike said.

'I said I had never *been* in,' said Kimiko.

'So, come in now and then you can never say you've never been again.'

So, in – much good objecting did me – we went. The bar was on the fourth floor. There was a lift at the end of the vestibule. *Lift?* A coffin on a rope. There were stairs. I went up by them. I might have been a pushover, but I wasn't a fool.

Despite its location off a landing in what appeared to be a converted department store, the bar was everything you would expect of an Irish bar abroad: a passage lined with Guinness barrels, leading under a slab of wood saying 'Fáilte' into a room dominated by a giant screen showing English Premiership football.

Before the screen a party of glazed-eyed businessmen sat at a round table balanced on another Guinness barrel, as though at a conference: 'The Effects on Conversation of Excessive Alcohol'. Profound. Silencing.

I found my own third party in a snug-like corner flanked by yet more barrels. The waiter was just leaving.

'I ordered you a stout,' Ike said.

'I never drink it.'

'I thought you'd say that, so I ordered you a whiskey too.'

The izakaya had been an exception. I didn't as a rule drink whiskey either. 'Thanks.'

A green baseball cap with the words 'Town Drunk' on the brow poked round the barrels, a face beneath it that made the cap look understated.

'Sorry.' American twang. 'I was looking for …' Eyes and tongue cast about, 'Shit.'

The cap took its face back. A bare two minutes later the waiter arrived with the drinks.

'Impossible,' Ike said. 'You can't pour four glasses of Guinness in that time. You can't pour one. You're meant to let it sit.'

The waiter smiled over the drinks' crew-cut heads. 'Good Guinness,' he said.

Ike grumbled. 'My father wouldn't even have accepted a glass of water that took less than five minutes to pour.'

We touched the lips of our glasses together, said the elephant thing. I had plumped for Guinness as marginally less evil in the circumstances than whiskey. I took a sip. Actually it tasted better than I had feared. Kimiko struggled to keep her eyebrows raised in pleasured surprise. Dražen set his glass down and nudged it with his fingernail a fraction closer to the centre of the table.

'So tell me,' I asked him, 'do you find a lot of Croatian bars on your travels?'

'Not so many, but then I do not look too hard.'

'Wise man.'

Ike took a long, leisurely drink, little finger cocked: this is water, this is a duck's back.

'People like you worry too much about this sort of thing,' he said.

'What do you mean, "people like me"?'

'I mean, there's a restaurant in Tokyo called Asia as Seen from Europe.'

'And what's *that* supposed to mean?'

'It means Irish Bar is another country, don't lose sleep about how they do things there.'

Sleep I could recover. It pained me to think how many business opportunities were lost in this Ireland of smoke and repro mirrors. I had heard there were Irish bars in the States that sold a cocktail called a car bomb. Let's drink one of those to your inward investment! Anyway, who was it was giving out this morning about god-awful Irish films?

'What was it like?' Kimiko asked.

'What?'

'Asia as Seen from Europe.'

'Great big Buddha, tons of candles, lots of Japanese people not fretting that they should have been eating in the Tokyo-as-seen-from-Tokyo restaurants up and down the street.'

'All right,' I said, 'point taken.'

I had had another taste of Guinness while he was talking: that slight sourness I remembered, but stomachable in small doses.

I edged my whiskey towards Dražen, who nodded gratefully. A sign over the window at his back said 'There are no strangers here, only friends who haven't met yet.' I thought of us all this morning at breakfast, not yet met. I thought of the buffet.

I stood up. 'Excuse me.'

Ike gave me the sly eye. 'You all right?'

'Fine. Toilet. That's all.'

I was fine, once I had put a bit of distance between my glass and me, and thoughts of more food. And I did have to go to the toilet. That was the way it came on me these days. Nought to sixty in seconds.

The round table before the giant screen was abandoned. The screen itself had switched allegiance, from English football to Dutch. PSV and some other set of initials I couldn't quite decipher.

I asked directions at the bar and followed the finger out, beneath the 'Fáilte', to a corridor facing the exit on to the fourth floor landing. There was a bit of sanctioned writing on the wall here, something about a pint of plain, just in case you weren't desperate enough already. I pushed the door open, looked in, and pulled it shut again. There was no mistaking that was the men's toilets. It was the men's toilets for all to see, inside this building and out, because the urinals backed on to a huge window, overlooking Chuo-dori. It was Hiroshima out there, ten-to-midnight busy. I contemplated the stairs behind me: half a minute and I would be at the taxi rank. But I could feel the pressure building. Even getting a taxi straightaway, I didn't know I would last the distance to the hotel.

I had no option. I opened the door again. There was Chuo-dori and there was the urinal. I stepped up to the mark. At least there were no windows facing me, just the rear end of Parco. And then, I wasn't entirely without cover. The porcelain was a solid slab: a waist-high headstone. I shrugged off a little of the hunch I had, without thinking, adopted. Down went the zip. Out came the pee, eventually. (That, after all the urgency, was also happening to me more and more.) It was a curious experience, then quite a fun one. I dinked my lad to the left to let the stream chase a white four-wheel drive off-screen; I dinked it right to sprinkle the satin jackets of the two Miami Vice throwbacks who had stopped by a street ashtray to light each other's cigarettes.

The door opened at my back. I peed straight, looking down, as though concentrating on the inscription. The cubicle door banged shut and the bolt slid across.

Twice I started to stop, then did stop, but knew enough not to move yet. I was waiting for the final trill, when I saw her on the pavement. The woman from the A-Bomb Museum. She must have stepped out from a building close at hand, or maybe she had been there all along and had only just then looked round. At least, I thought she had looked round, for all I could see now was the back of her head, her shoulders. But it was her. I would have bet my life on it. I shook my lad; throttled it.

'Come on,' I said and gritted my teeth.

The man in the cubicle coughed. There was a splash. I managed a few drops. I was standing on tiptoe. I lost her for a moment in Chuo-dori's human traffic then I picked her up again, right on the edge of the kerb, stepping out from the magnolias. I thumped the window with the heel of my hand.

'Wait!'

And then I saw the man. He had been bending over to speak into a taxi. He straightened now (glasses? he didn't have glasses in the museum); beckoned to her.

I fumbled myself back into my shorts, hit the window again. '*Wait!*'

The woman walked to the taxi. It was pulling away almost as soon as she was in the door.

'No!' I cried, and that was when the pee came, a thimbleful, no more, but a thimbleful in the confines of my shorts. I made a dash for the paper towels. The toilet behind the cubicle door flushed. When the man emerged I was stuffing a towel through my open zip, trying to stem the trickle that was working its way down my trouser leg. It was the Town Drunk. He looked at me as though the hat was on my head. When he had washed his hands (for he was a meticulous drunk, I'll give him that) I rested my head on the towel dispenser and screamed.

The glasses – it wasn't the same man. She had taken the final step. If that was her, getting into the taxi. I was four floors up. I had only seen her face for a fraction of a second, but I wouldn't have forgotten it so soon. Would I?

The door opened. A snarly snatch of Oasis. Dražen came in.

'Who took the wall away?' he asked, then pointed at the front of my trousers. 'Everything is OK?'

'The taps.' I slipped off my jacket and folded it over my arm for cover. 'They spray everywhere.'

He walked to the window. He said something, something Cravat, I thought. He turned to me smiling, his hand on his belt.

'What do you say? Two moons over Hiroshima.'

'God's sake, Dražen!' He had the trousers half down, 'Don't. You'll get us …'

Arrested, I was going to say, then was pulled up by what I saw: a patch of yellow skin high up on his right inner thigh, stretched-looking, hairless. Graft. I would have put money on it. He hitched the trousers back up to below his hips, holding them closed with his fist.

'I thought that was tradition,' he said, and took himself off to the cubicle.

I had my hand on the door to leave when I thought, we're all drunk, it's now or never.

'Dražen? What was it you did?'

'Did?' He was obviously confused by the tense as much as the context. So I told him about this morning, as he was leaving the breakfast room, Ike saying he was a national hero.

'I did not do anything unusual. I write like I always write, criticisms. Only the times are unusual. I was arrested. Then there is nothing I can do even for myself.'

'I'm sorry.'

'Please.' His voice was strained. 'Can you go?'

I opened the door. I caught only a little of his sigh in the lull before the next song: some old garbage with fiddles that had them whooping and cheering across the border in Irish Bar. I crossed over myself. A few people, encouraged by the fiddles, were making flat-footed shapes at one another. The Dutch initials were chasing each other around, pointlessly, the box in the corner of the screen confirmed.

Ike was leaning in close to Kimiko when I came round the corner, one hand on the barrel by her head. There was inevitability about it. Even so, the sight of them, so soon after seeing that taxi drive away, left me utterly bereft. I took a step backwards. She looked up; he looked round. Her face was glum, his triumphant.

'Tell him,' he said to her.

'Tell me what?'

Kimiko shrugged. 'There are no eagles in Hiroshima.'

'What did I say? No eagles.'

'I used to believe in such fantastical things,' said Kimiko, 'but not any more.'

'Maybe it was lost,' I said. 'Or just passing through.'

'Maybe.' She sounded genuinely crestfallen. 'More likely it was a crow. We have very large crows.'

'I know crows and I know what I saw.'

'Good for you.' Her face, like her voice, brightened a little. I went to say more then realised Dražen was behind me.

'There is a woman dancing on the landing,' he said. 'All by herself.'

Kimiko stood up. 'I want to see.'

Ike seemed surprised by the sudden movement, but turned sideways in his seat to let her pass.

'Are you coming?' Dražen asked.

'I'll wait for the report,' he said. He had finished his own Guinness and made a start on Dražen's.

'Well?' I sat across from him, jacket on my lap. I could see the back of his head in the window. His hair was definitely going. 'Are you satisfied?'

He smacked his lips. 'Yep.' The fiddles were doing ninety. 'No eagles.'

'I don't even think you care about being right, just as long as I'm wrong.'

'No, being right's good too.'

Suddenly Irish Bar did not seem quite so foreign, or fake. I remembered from my teen years how, late in a night's drinking, fights could flare between even the firmest friends, but how too in every group there seemed always to be a couple of guys sniping at each other, who would last be seen walking off up the road together, sharing a bag of chips. That would be Ike and me, going home.

I took a drink. It was that or telling him in a chip-sharing sort of way he was a complete and utter bastard.

A complete and utter bastard whose autograph I had been tasked with bringing back to Belfast. No better time than this to ask, the two of us sitting here on our own. And yet I didn't want him – or me – feeling I was all take and no give. Instinct bade me trade. I cleared my throat to break the silence we had lapsed into.

'That story I was telling you about?'

He sat forward, quicker, on reflection, than he wanted to be seen to, and sank back again. 'What about it?'

'Well, the day I was to leave Tokyo for here, something came up. Bags packed, bill paid and everything and suddenly I'm not going till the next day. I'd the hotel and all booked here, you understand, so I just thought, I'll not bother ringing to cancel, I'll be charged for it whatever happens, and anyway, tomorrow morning when I arrive I can just go straight in, unpack, get a shower if I need it, instead of hanging round waiting on the room being made up. So, well and good, I get in mid-morning and walk up to the desk …'

Dražen appeared, reaching for his whiskey, his face, his gestures, saying sorry for interrupting. I couldn't see, but it sounded as though the jigging had spread into the bar: a lot of toes inexpertly tapping.

'And?' said Ike.

'And I walked up to the desk and says to the guy, I want to check in, and then explained about what had happened the night before. So he types away on his computer and then hits the same key a couple of times and frowns and types a bit more. Here he is: I'm sorry we don't have a room ready at the moment. If you'd like to have a coffee in the lounge …

'I says, Hold on. Not ready? My room must be ready: there was nobody in it last night.

'He shakes his head. Here he is: What room?

'Here's me: What room do you think? The room I booked.

'So then he smiles, like I'm a child needs all this explained to me. Here he is: The room is not there until you check in. Here's me to him: Sure I *paid* for it. How can I pay for a room that isn't there? He gives me the wee smile again and here he's to me: If you had been here then the room would have been, but you were not so the room was not.'

Ike was looking across the table at me, expression as vacant as the room I hadn't slept in.

'You're allowed to speak now,' I told him. 'I'm finished.'

He stared a moment or two longer then shook himself. 'That's not it,' he said.

I laughed. 'Of course it's it. It's my story, I should know.'

'Nobody in their right mind would call that great.'

'Maybe not on its own, but it could be the start of something: The Room That Never Was. You're the writer.' I almost felt sorry for him, he looked so annoyed. 'I told you this morning, you probably had to be there.'

He drank the remains of Dražen's Guinness. Well-poured or not, there was still that familiar nylons-slide of dregs down the inside of the glass. He struck the base on the table edge.

'There's something else you're not telling me.'

I laughed again, but it sounded wrong.

'Definitely.' He nodded, as though that settled matters. 'I've thought it all along.'

Kimiko and Dražen returned. There was a heat off them, like the dancing had overtaken them too. I took advantage of the diversion they created.

'I really should make a move,' I said.

'We all should,' said Kimiko, but no one else did and I wondered if I wasn't expected to bring proceedings to a more formal close. I remembered Ike's toast in the izakaya. 'Drink?' I asked.

Kimiko looked sick at the prospect. Dražen's hand closed like a lid on his glass. Even Ike shook his head, scowling.

'Well, then, thanks a million for having me along this evening. Not what I had in mind when I woke up this morning, but I wouldn't have missed it for anything.'

I offered my hand all round the table. Light shake, firm shake, cold shake.

'You've got my card. Next time you can all be my guests. Maybe in Belfast … the next book launch?'

Dražen and Kimiko stole quick sideways glances at Ike then both looked down at the table. I knew nothing about writing, but I knew how to read a look. The revenge of the back-to-front horse: there was no next book, no *Hurts 2*, no *Bitter End* even.

'Oh,' I said. 'Right. Sorry.'

'Go fuck yourself,' Ike said quietly.

'Easy on there, I said I was sorry.'

'You? Sorry for me? That's a good one.'

'I just got the impression you were a bit …'

'A bit what?' He was on his feet.

'Nothing.'

'I'm a bit fed up with you is what I am, more than a bit. I've had it up to here.' He had to tilt his chin to keep it above the line drawn by his right hand. Behind him, and keeping time, a vast electronic hoarding filled with corporate orange. 'I've seen you, don't worry, all those wee smirks of yours.'

Me smirking?

'Listen,' I said, 'it doesn't matter what I say here. You've decided you're going to be offended. I shouldn't have spoken. I shouldn't have come out. I should have sat where I was this morning eating my breakfast. They're two different worlds yours and mine. Half the time I'm not even sure we live in the same city.'

There was a beat then he lunged across the table at me. Dražen hauled him back.

'Get your hands off me,' Ike shouted. I fell back into my seat, astonished. He grabbed the flight bag and shoved the table with his thighs, slopping drinks.

'Wait,' I said, but he was off round the corner and gone.

'Bloody hell,' I said then. 'What was all that about?'

Dražen and Kimiko stared at me a moment in silence.

'I should go after him,' Kimiko said.

Dražen took her hand. 'No, the walk will do him good. He will find his way.'

'You act as though he does this all the time,' I said.

'Now and then,' Dražen said, then revised it: 'More and more.'

'But he's still doing all right, isn't he? I mean there were fellas tonight inviting him to *Rio*.'

'I think,' said Dražen, 'he is afraid of running out of places to go.'

'I don't understand.'

'Passage he read this evening? Is passage he always reads. People queue up, they buy the book. It is not so easy as the passage they heard; they read, they read, waiting for this passage, but by the time they get there they are already bored from looking and he is already on plane somewhere else, where he reads his passage and people queue up ...' He turned, as he said this, to Kimiko. 'He will tell you himself.'

Kimiko hadn't withdrawn her hand. He stroked her knuckles with the pad of his thumb. I had made more than one misjudgement, it seemed. I stood up again.

'Excuse me, I have to go.' They didn't try to persuade me to stay.

Out on the landing the lift door was about to close on a couple French kissing. I took a breath for courage and leapt in beside them. Any tighter in there we'd have been exchanging numbers when the door opened again on the ground floor. I left them still tongue-tied and belted out on to the street. Forget the taxis. Dražen had said 'walk'; he knew him of old. I looked this way and that. That, definitely.

The shutters were coming down on a pachinko parlour I passed, to the regular closing-time accompaniment of 'Auld Lang Syne'. Every night an Old You's Night and a Luckier New You every day.

I never once doubted my own luck the whole Ike-less length of Chuo-dori. I caught up with him a block short of the avenue's end, outside a darts bar. He had been struggling with something in his jacket pocket – the notebook maybe – but gave up when he saw me and carried on walking. I matched him step for step.

'Another story,' I said. 'The one I should have told you.' And without even asking myself why I was doing it I started in about the A-Bomb Museum and the woman in the vest top and going back a third time hoping to meet her and to hell with ever going home again. I told him how at moments today I had felt I was watching my life rather than living it, as though I had left a door open between one way of going on and another.

I finished with me back there in the toilets of the Irish bar, banging the window, even though I think I knew it wasn't her getting into the taxi below me. Only conference-goers and mayor-stalkers stayed in Hiroshima more than a day or two.

We were within sight of our hotel now, passing a gallery whose single display, stretched at an angle on the floor, was a band of white silk, from which human figures had been cut, or blasted, as it looked: sticking to the walls, leaving hands, feet, whole limbs behind.

Ike walked a few yards more in silence, then, 'No,' he said. 'No?'

'That's not it either.' It was said without aggression, it's true, but it was the last straw for me.

'Right, forget it,' I said. I strode on ahead.

He called after me. 'Thanks for trying all the same.'

I threw a hand up behind my head, three fingers short of a wave.

I was already in the lift when he came into the lobby and walked up to reception. I pressed number twenty-three repeatedly and hard. I needn't have worried. As the doors closed I saw him hunched over the desk, still talking to the night clerk.

Bye, then, I thought. And then I thought, no autograph.

2

I couldn't believe the stuff lying about the place. (Had the room got untidier while I was out?) I couldn't believe the time. Another hour finagled from me. I sat on the bed and laid each ankle in turn upon the opposite knee to undo my laces. Actually removing the blasted shoes was too much of an effort. I lay back, feet planted on the floor. The room shifted a little on its axis. I sat up. Something rustled in my trousers. I pulled my zip to half-mast and fished in my shorts: the paper towel from the bar. I balled it up and tossed it towards the bin. Missed. I shook my head at myself from way at the back of the dressing table mirror.

Honestly, the state of you.

I forced myself to stand. Water, that's what I needed. I opened one of the bottles from the minibar and tipped my head back. What ran down my chin alone cost more than bottles twice the size in the convenience store round the corner. When I had finished I went back to the fridge for the other bottle.

With the work I had done since I had been here the board could absorb one more.

Slowly I began to re-fold the clothes strewn on the bed, telling myself proper packing always stands to you. No matter how tired I was, I would be glad when I got home I had taken the trouble.

I checked my email one last time – no acknowledgement from Tom; not even Norma had been able to raise herself – and switched off the laptop. I had zipped two sides of its carry-case when I stopped. A knock, it sounded like. I looked over my shoulder at the door. There was still a television on somewhere along the corridor. I listened for sounds that weren't it then went back to the laptop case … turned again almost immediately. No mistaking it this time: a knock.

It could only be one person.

I didn't say a word, but tiptoed across the floor, stopping at every creak, picking my spot carefully to begin again. Once, I overbalanced, but managed to right myself using only my fingertips, noiseless against the wall; picked my spot, began again. At last I stood with my ear to the door. I held my breath … Not a sound. I risked a peek through the spy-hole. Not a sinner. So of course I opened the door then. How *dare* there be nobody there after all that?

The corridor was two walls looking blankly at each other. I was about to leave them to it when my eye lit on the book lying in front of my door. *Hurts*: his own copy, complete with Post Its. I hunkered down to look at it. 'Astonishing,' said the *Independent* on the front cover.

He couldn't have just dropped it. Drop it and you would be chasing pages all over the corridor. It had to have been left there deliberately. I turned it over with my index finger, still on my guard for unpleasant surprises. 'Powerful,' said the *Scotsman*.

I picked the book up and brought it into the room.

The inside page was dense with more quotes: *The Times*, the *Mail*, the *Observer*, the *Sunday Business Post*, *GQ*, and most of the ones starting with *Irish*. The page after that was blank, the one after that had his signature, followed by a PS: 'We're having a <u>last</u> last drink. Come on ahead down.'

I lowered myself on to the bed and turned the page again, to the first page proper. Ten lines in there was the name of a shop that closed when I was still in primary school. A tanning studio now. No, wait. I looked in the mirror again, reading my lips. Next to the tanning studio: a discount bookstore, of all things. Would he have known? He must have known. That was probably why ... I was on to the next page before the words of that one had sunk in. I went back to the start, went forward more slowly, skipping over the odd line I had actually got on first reading. A couple of pages further on I started flicking through, hunting for the passage he had read at the university, then realised what I was doing and flicked back to the dedication. I could hardly give this to Tom and Jill. 'We're having a <u>last</u> last drink.'

I aligned the loose pages and laid the book face down on my lap.

We?

It didn't seem likely that Dražen and Kimiko would have come back, not the way I had left them, hand in hand, in the Irish bar, or if they had, that they would have wanted any company but their own. I sat a while. It bothered me. We.

I walked to the door again. I watched my hand reach out and hover just short of the handle. For the first time it occurred to me that the consequences of my decision could be irreversible. I imagined the PA in the departure lounge: This is a third and final call for passenger ... Me still somewhere between here and there.

I could walk back to the bed right now, wriggle between the covers, get a couple of hours' sleep before the alarm.

We.

I opened the door and stepped outside: the two walls, the vague hum of all-night lighting, the solitary TV, who knows where.

Halfway down the corridor I almost lost one of my shoes. I had forgotten to redo the laces. I bent to tie them and only then realised I still had the book in my left hand. It was as far to go back as it was to go forward to the lifts. I went forward.

Sure enough the panel above the lift on the left was showing Ike's floor number. The lift stirred into life the instant I pressed the up arrow – no competing claims at this hour – and drew back its door to reveal a refurbished interior: padded leather hand rail where once there was brass; mink and cream carpet instead of emerald green.

I pressed nineteen. The lift went up to twenty-five, the Skylight restaurant and bar. I shrank back against the rail as the door opened. Across the landing were double glass doors, tables running away from them into the gloom of the empty restaurant, like the islands disappearing in the haze of the Inland Sea; then there was another pinpoint of light, faint, orange, corresponding to the bar area. I had a good five seconds in which to observe it. It didn't move. The door closed, the lift descended without further bidding. It stopped, such is the logic of lifts, on my floor, confirmed I wasn't still out there waiting, and carried on down.

Nineteen – such was the logic of the Hana's management – had already been renovated, its decor an outpouring of the lift that had brought me there. It was all more subdued than my own floor; even the inevitable rogue TV sounded muffled. But there was, I noticed the second after the lift door shut, another sound below that, boiler-roomish, bowelly. I looked behind me.

The door on to the stairs beside the right-hand lift was open, pushed back on its hinges by a cleaning cart. All tomorrow's bed-sheets neatly pressed and stacked. I listened at the threshold a few moments. Nothing but the throb of pipes far, far below. A sign on the stairwell pointed back the way I had come to the Skylight restaurant and bar, for anyone health-conscious, or claustrophobic, enough to be walking. The emergency exit sign, above the door itself, reminded me that this was in fact a fire door and should not be open at all. I didn't think twice. I eased the cart further into the stairwell with my toe and let the door swing shut.

There was a moan, coming from or connected to the TV, otherwise the only sound now was my footsteps going against the grain of the new carpet.

I remembered the drag of Ike's feet, the night I helped him back to his room, his all-too-tangible weight on my shoulders, and I realised there was every chance that he had not really gone astray, but had in his drunken way been seeking me out even then.

I stopped outside his door. The lock was not properly engaged. My light knock unhoused it completely. I waited for an invitation to enter then knocked again. The door opened wider. I glimpsed a glass of beer half-drunk on the console of the bathroom sink, a sticky lip print on the rim.

'Hello?' I said.

I was in the hall now. The only light here was from the bathroom. A wooden luggage rack stood between it and the closet. Two photographs lay on the rack's canvas straps. I glanced at the top one. Ike and Tadao at Mount Ogon-zan. Instantly I saw what it was that had eluded me this morning: the shinkansen in the background looked as though it was burrowing from the left ear of one into the right ear of the other. But there was something else odd. I peered more closely. Tadao's gesture … My heart gave a lurch.

I called Ike's name, loud.

'I was beginning to think you weren't going to make it,' he said.

I still couldn't see him. 'I'm sorry I got a bit … lost.' One word fits all, book and lift. I came right into the room.

'It's all right,' he said. 'We've had plenty to occupy us.'

He was sitting on the far side of the bed at the table before the window. A table-lamp cast a circle of yellow light downwards on bottles from the minibar and a smaller circle upwards on

Tadao, looking at me with barely disguised hostility: the day's mask slipped.

I was trying to work out how to take Ike aside, ask him had he had a good look at that photo, the way Tadao's fingers were turned, but there was something else Ike was looking at, a little silver compact, open in his right palm.

'Tadao here has been showing me his phone. Amazing the things you can do with it. Just amazing.'

I didn't want to take my eye off Tadao. There was no knowing what he might do or when. And yet, it was hard not to be distracted by the glow of the tiny screen, to try to make sense of the half-glimpsed images.

'Like, you take this stuff. He was able to get all this off the internet when he was home printing out the photos for me. Imagine, I have to travel half the world to read my local paper.'

As soon as I realised what Tadao had been at I could pretty much fill in the detail of what was on the screen, the picture carried by some of our papers when the Sardinia business first surfaced, of a dark-eyed child in his mother's arms. 'Hidden victim of our messy peace' was one caption I remembered.

'I know it looks bad,' I said, 'but it wasn't our fault.'

'No' – Ike pressed a key that caused the phone to beep, pressed the one he ought to have pressed the first time and text appeared – 'I think what the judge says here is that he was sorry he couldn't say for definite it was your fault. "How sad, though, that the shady dealings of a country a thousand miles away should be visited with such misery on our own children."'

There had been an error in the composition of the film for our U-bag prototype. Not enough of the soya oil compound that kept the plastic chemically stable and prevented the phthalates from leeching. Don't ask me how much we were short (don't ask me what a phthalate is): a tiny, tiny bit, though of course we decided, the instant we discovered the error, to scrap the entire batch. Three years of research and development down the tubes. Three years and I shuddered still to think how

159

many hundreds of thousands of pounds. I was asked to handle the tenders for the disposal. I wasn't told to go for the cheapest, but after the hammering we had already taken I would have had to make a pretty good case for going for anyone else. A vague suspicion about a company's origins did not seem to me a pretty good case. Waste disposal is not a business you want to go sniffing around in too much in Northern Ireland. Besides, it was listed in the companies' registry.

'The best thing out of Belfast since the wheel,' Ike sneered.

I wrote to the board recommending we accept the tender.

The film was taken away in a container, but was not destroyed as agreed. Instead the container was shipped to Sardinia, where the cargo was sold on to another firm who repackaged it and sold it as bona fide clingfilm. It was a year before the effects became apparent: a cluster of baby boys in the north of the island born with hypospadias. (I had to look that one up too: the opening of the penis in the wrong place.) It was another six months before the connection was made with the clingfilm. The Sardinians involved were quickly arrested, but the Belfast waste disposal firm was gone, its managing director gone with it, to Spain, pursued by two extradition requests, one from the Sardinian authorities, one from our own Assets Recovery Agency. The man who had signed himself 'Esq.' in his letters to me was better known to the police and his balaclava buddies as Brigadier. The light shone briefly, but unkindly, on our company.

'The best thing out of Belfast since the wheel!' Ike gave the sneer another spin. 'Pass me a U-bag, I'm going to be sick.'

'The board voted over fifty thousand pounds to pay for surgery,' I said.

'Where surgery is possible,' he shot back.

'In most cases it will be.'

'Most.'

'Nearly all.'

'Nearly.'

They ruin us and then feel good for treating us. Except I didn't feel good, I didn't feel good at all. I didn't say anything for a moment. When I spoke next I directed my gaze at Ike alone.

'I think you had better be careful.'

He sat forward. 'Is that a threat?'

'There's no threat from me.'

'Who, then? Tadao here?'

'It's him has been doing all that graffiti.'

Ike looked at Tadao, who shook his head, as well he might.

'He's been tailing you. That time you were in Limerick, the reading with the riot. He was at it. Ask him.'

'I don't need to,' Ike said. 'I haven't been in Limerick for ten years. More. Tadao was barely out of short trousers.'

That stumped me, but it didn't stop me. 'Look at the photograph I took this morning, that's all I'm saying.'

'I've looked at it.'

'And?'

'I look old and he looks a prick, like I warned him he would.'

'He's making a gun, not a peace sign.'

'I scratched my head as you took the photo,' said Tadao.

'And,' I talked over him, 'he was at the taxis when Kimiko was getting in. That note in her bag ...'

'I'm fucking sick saying it.' Ike threw up his hands. The phone flew out and landed face down on the bed. Tadao started forward; sat back. 'The graffiti is a joke. There is no big conspiracy. You ask me, you've been reading the wrong books.'

I suppose the *Iliad* would have explained everything.

'You ask me,' I said, 'you shouldn't be so quick to judge.'

'Oh?' That supercilious expression of his. 'Surprise me, then. What *have* you been reading?'

We were back to day one again, 'Tell me the novels you've heard of ...'

The year before last I had joined a world classics club, but had left after only a month. They let me keep the signing-on gift. *Don Quixote*. A sash across the front told me it was the only novel I would ever need. I brought it with me on all my trips. I was only a couple of hundred pages in, but I would still have bluffed it out, if I had just been a bit more certain about how to pronounce the name. *Quicks–? Keyho–?*

'I've read enough,' I said, lamely, I knew.

He stood up, shook a can of tonic, and walked to the minibar.

'Drink?' he said to Tadao, not to me.

I was still holding the copy of *Hurts*.

'You'll probably want this back,' I said.

'Do you know what? You keep it.' He flicked his fingers towards me, as though shaking off dirt. 'Now, go.'

I started to say again that he was getting me, getting the company, all wrong, but he wasn't having any of it.

'Are you deaf as well as crooked? I said *go*.'

I stumbled down the dark hallway and into the corridor. I didn't know there was anyone at my back till I turned at the door just as Tadao slammed it in my face. I leaned against the wall outside, trying to steady my breathing. Fuck you. Fuck you. Fuck. You.

I brought my children up to understand that the first time either of them swore at me would be their last time. The night Tom chanced it I chased him up the stairs and along the landing to his bedroom. He got the door shut a breath before I could grab a hold of him and trail him back downstairs. I pushed at the door till it nearly buckled. The weight was all at the bottom. He was sitting with his back to it.

'I'll give you to the count of three to open this door.'

'Aye, so you can hit me?'

'I won't hit you.'

'You will.'

'I will if you don't open it. One …' I wasn't sure what I would do: kick the door; take a run and thump it with my shoulder;

turn the handle and hope he had been scared enough to move. 'Two ...'

He opened the door. He had been crying.

'Never you speak to me like that again.'

'Or what, you'll get the boys round?'

I hit him.

'You couldn't leave it, could you?' I shouted.

He turned and walked into the room and lay down on the bed with his face to the wall. That was something I had never understood till then myself: the first time you hit a child like that might as well be the last. You can't beat the lost respect back into them.

My wife went up to him a couple of hours later. 'You don't realise what it's like to be a parent,' she said.

'Don't give me that did-it-all-for-us crap.'

'Your dad didn't *do* anything. It was an honest mistake, it could have happened to anyone here.'

'Well then, the whole place stinks,' he said. 'I want nothing more to do with it.'

He recovered quickly enough, though, once he was across the water.

'It's wonderful what a bit of sea can do,' my wife said.

His phone calls from college were shopping lists. It was a business arrangement. So-many-hundred pounds spent on this item or that bought me so-many son-hours, as though he had decided if it *had* all been for him, then that was the least he could reasonably be expected to settle for: it all.

At least Tom talked to me. Jill preferred to spin out her wants and woes along the worldwide web. She preferred, when the option was there, not to sleep under the same roof as her mother and me, or that was how it was starting to look.

'She'll come round too,' my wife said one night in bed. 'Anyway, there are two girls in her class whose daddies are estate agents.'

The head of a local agency had been arrested earlier in the

week on suspicion of laundering paramilitary cash.

'That doesn't make me feel a whole lot better.'

She moved her hand under the covers. 'I know what would.'

We hadn't had too many moments like that in the previous few months. Once it's in there, hypospadias is a hard word to get out of your head.

But then – she was unbuttoning my pyjama top – there comes a time – kissing down my chest, on to my stomach – you try to put these things behind you. What choice – pyjama bottoms undone – do you have?

Take a deep breath. Go on.

3

I was walking back along the corridor to the lifts when I remembered the girl. Mami.

Of course. The third glass, by the bathroom sink, in Ike's room.

I looked at the fire door and the cleaning cart behind it. I opened the door a fraction, listening for sounds above me rather than below. I let it close again. I contemplated the lift. The lift that had taken me up before it would bring me down. I couldn't quite get the measure of this – the *trigonometry* – though I was in no doubt that everything pointed to her, up there.

The lift hadn't gone anywhere while I had been in the room. It opened almost before my finger touched the button. I got in, reached out for number twenty-three, then reached higher: twenty-five.

I barely had time to brace myself against the rail, much less plan my next move, before the lift door opened again, too soon and too late. The faint orange dot I had seen last time had faded completely. I could scarcely even imagine now where it had been. *If* it had.

I crossed the landing floor like I was crossing ice, conscious suddenly of the empty rooms below me, the painters' sheets settled soft as silt over every surface. It was a relief to reach the restaurant doors, and no surprise at all to find them unlocked. As quickly as it had welled, my uncertainty receded.

Wrong books, Ike? You think so?

The air inside was heavy with the smell of disinfectant spray. I felt my way forward, bumping against chairs, righting them, until I got a whiff of something unsuppressed, something *subsequent* to the spray, something that only gradually took on the character of smoke. I followed my nose to where the smell was strongest, the table by the window with the ashtray six inches off-centre.

I pinched the butt between my thumb and forefinger, a tight scroll of cardboard. Not a cigarette, a joint, the faintest trace of lip-gloss close to the end. I put it to my own lips and inhaled. Dead ash and bubblegum.

Where are you?

I pulled out a chair and sat. I thought I would give it a minute, see would she come back, ask her what this was all about. Kobe, maybe, or maybe it was losing her man to him, mind if not body. Tadao was not the culprit. Tadao was the cover.

The sap.

I don't know if it was the ghost of the joint working on me, but I didn't feel the least bit anxious any more. I lay my head on the table, looking out. To the right the night was a huge nothing into which yesterday had disappeared. To the left it was split by a wafer-thin light, like a lid lifted on tomorrow. I closed one eye to give the sky the window to itself, opened that eye and closed the other to bring the ashtray centre-frame.

The ashtray was sitting a fraction higher at one side. I nudged it and uncovered a pale thread; tugged the thread and pulled out a sewing needle. I raised my head, holding the thread up before me. The needle twirled and as I followed its movement Mami was conjured for me in all her chaotic detail. The hat, the neckerchiefs, the row of needles in the lapel, from which this must have come ...

The needle twirled.

I couldn't tear my eyes away, couldn't even blink. The bangles, the bag, *the badges.* A spaced-out eagle and a defenestrated man.

The needle stopped twirling. I didn't blink.

And still I didn't. And still.

All at once the feeling came on me. I had to go. Really, really had to go. Not even seconds to decide. Now.

I picked up the book and started walking back towards the restaurant doors, moving chairs aside as I went, clearing my path, ten paces, fifteen paces, twenty. Then I turned and charged. *Twentyfifteenten* ... I dipped as I closed in on the table, catching it with my midriff, shoving it like a ram before me, but the legs snagged on the carpet, or snapped or something, and the table flipped up, catapulting me clean through the glass as though it wasn't there.

The ultimate pun and no one to inflict it on: it was just like the song said, paneless.

Ropeless.

For a single, pure breath more I was still travelling forwards. Then I wasn't. The weight of my body seemed to rip right past me, the flesh of sixteen thousand days compounded: my balls were boulders, my heart was a whole house of hearts, my ears were ferry doors flapping open. The last ounce I knew would sink my soul, then, at the very moment that the drag became irresistible, a shadow swooped and, with an ease bred of aeons, talons reached right in and plucked me free. I looked down and there was the husk of me, without the wit to quit, pedalling the air, like a trick-cyclist, arms shot straight up from the shoulders.

The book left the hand that was holding it surprisingly late. The pages flew upwards, still in sequence, before fanning out, creating their own little storm.

'Astonishing.'

'Powerful.'

The husk jerked – the bike whipped from under it – then stopped resisting.

And the further from view it fell the more clearly I saw everything else. I saw Mami pressed against a window on the stairs from the twenty-fifth floor, one hand raised reflexively somewhere between *Stop!* and a simple wave goodbye. I saw Tadao, belatedly wondering where she had got to, tear himself from Ike's side and go searching the corridors for her. I saw Dražen and Kimiko, down by the river, not letting go of the night. I saw the crane behind the bus shelter, head tucked under its wing. I saw, having no control in this either, the Portaloos on Ogon-zan, the plane I wouldn't catch, the plane that would eventually carry what they thought was me home. I saw it all, and all at once, as though the talons were carrying me not on, or up, but beyond, to where time ceased to have meaning.

I saw the husk become a speck and disappear without a sound through the canopy of the ornamental gardens. I saw a taxi come round the curve of the access road. No one got out, no one came out.

Then everyone was running everywhere, everywhen.

I saw the last of the pages drift to the ground even as the police, their examination of them completed, were adding two and two and getting Ike, even as he was coming to the door in answer to their knock, haggard, in his black suit, as a man who has walked out of his own wake, even as they were sitting him down in the lounge, next to the Pianola, and asking him to tell them the whole story.

You'll be sorry, I thought, as the wings above me beat. Or I will be. But, then, I thought, No, let them.

Let him.

Acknowledgements

Thanks to the Arts Council of Northern Ireland and the British Council for their financial assistance during the writing of this novel. Thanks to all those who helped and advised me here and in Japan, especially David Burleigh, Andrew Fitzsimons, Liam Heggarty, Hiroko Ikeda, Yuriko Kobayashi, Suzanne McMillan, Chris Moore, Hitomi Nagahori, Kaori Nakasu, Mina Takahashi, and Masahiko Yahata. If I have gone wrong anywhere it is through no fault of theirs. Thanks also to the Japan branch of the International Association for the Study of Irish Literatures and to Matthew Sweeney for being such good company.

Thanks, finally, to Antony Harwood and James Macdonald Lockhart for their unwavering support, and to Patsy Horton and Anne Tannahill, book-lovers first and foremost.

Coming soon from
Blackstaff Press

GLENN PATTERSON

Burning Your Own

'Remarkably assured . . . Patterson's novel, needless to say,
is neither afraid nor prejudiced, but courageously
magnanimous.'

GUARDIAN

'a passionately engaged portrayal of a troubled boy
and city'

OBSERVER

ISBN 978-0-85640-810-6

£6.99

www.blackstaffpress.com

Coming soon from
Blackstaff Press

GLENN PATTERSON
The International

'Glenn Patterson has become the most serious and humane
chronicler of Northern Ireland over the past thirty years, as well as
one of the best contemporary Irish novelists.'

COLM TÓIBÍN

'A funny, moving, politically astute novel rooted in the
last three decades of Belfast's history. Beautifully observed and
crafted, I'd recommend it to anyone who values
honest prose.'

A.L. KENNEDY

ISBN 978-0-85640-812-0
£6.99

www.blackstaffpress.com